I0623518

Naughty

and

Nice

Naughty and Nice

Candice Bradford

Bradbury Stone

Toby Kent

Marlena Wolf

Amethyst Bercher

Copyright © 2018 Wolfstone Books
All rights reserved.
ISBN-13: 978-1-925892-03-1
No portion of this book may be reproduced or used in any manner
whatsoever without the express written permission of the publisher,
except for the use of brief quotations in a book review.
For more information, please contact Marlena Wolf via our website
or at PO Box 9 Buxton NSW Australia 2571

For Miesha

Dear Reader,

Thank you for choosing to spend some time with a Wolfstone book.

We do hope you enjoy reading it as much as we enjoyed writing it.

Why not visit our webpage www.wolfstone.com.au for all our social media contacts, our contact form or to tell us you have spotted a typo.

While you're there, you can join our mailing list to be kept up to date with all the latest news and new releases.

We love to hear from our fans so don't be shy. Tell us what you like so we can give you more!

Rather wait until the end of the book to see if you like us? No problem we will put the details there too, just for you xx

This book is entirely a work of fiction. Any resemblance to real people or situations is purely coincidental. It contains graphic content of a sexual nature and is for the entertainment of people over the age of 18 years only.

All of our characters, whilst fictional, are consenting adults.

Contents

Mr. and Mrs. Claus

There was something about the staff Christmas party that always made Sally feel like she was part of a big family. Something she needed more than ever this year. She had been with the company since she left school and, for the last five years, had been assistant to the boss. Three years with Mr. Joel Brennan Senior and then the last two years with Joel Junior. She loved her job.

One of her favourite parts of her job was dressing up as Mrs. Claus to the Boss's Santa and helping give out the gifts she had carefully chosen for the staff in the weeks leading up to the party.

Her bright red, sleeveless dress had the traditional white fur trim and a flounced skirt with built-in white mesh petticoats. Her bright red socks were pulled up to well above the knee and held snuggly to just below her mid-thigh. She wore a small Santa style hat, carefully bobby-pinned to her hair, and her favourite pair of winter boots which would normally be far too hot for this time of year, but they always had the air-conditioning set pretty cool for the Christmas party so that people didn't 'melt' in the hot Sydney weather.

The photographer set up a blue backdrop behind Santa's throne and put fake snow blowers either side. So white fluff was blown across as each member of staff had their Christmas photo taken with Mr. and Mrs. Claus.

She was feeling the need to brighten herself up a bit this year, so her costume was a little cheekier than usual. So much so that she had to be mindful of how she bent to lift the gifts to hand to Santa and, after a while, everybody could see her dilemma - and frequently her underwear. It became quite the joke. But it was all in fun and Sally was enjoying herself immensely, watching people open the gifts that were sometimes humorous, sometimes serious, but always bought with thought and care.

One of the other things she loved about her job was the way that their boss, Joel, was always the last to leave the party. He never left until after he made sure he handed an envelope containing a hand-written Christmas card and a cash bonus to each of the cleaning, catering, and security staff. He thanked them all personally for working late on Christmas Eve and wished them each a Merry Christmas before he retired to his office for a nightcap.

It had been a fantastic night and had taken Sally's mind off her troubles and made her feel quite cheerful. She smiled at Joel as he did his rounds, then walked back to the office with him to get her clothes to change out of her costume and head home.

"Do you have to rush away tonight Sal? Want to join me for a drink?" Joel asked with a charming smile when they got back to her desk.

Usually Sally had family commitments at Christmas, but not this time. Her brother was working in Japan for a year and her parents had flown out the week before to spend Christmas with him and have a few weeks holiday. So, she was in no hurry to be going home to an empty house. The idea of spending Christmas day alone for the first time in her life was like a looming black cloud. She was trying to be sanguine about it, but she was not looking forward to it at all.

"Yes, thanks, Joel. I'd love a drink."

He held open his office door for her and headed to the bottom cupboard in the bar behind his desk. He pulled out the good stuff usually reserved for extremely long-standing clients or for when his father popped in 'just to say hello'. The old man missed his job, but his health had forced him to retire sooner than he planned, thrusting Joel into the top job a long time before he was expecting it. But it was as if he was born to it. The transition went very smoothly.

"All thanks to Sally," he would say when people commented on his success, and she would always blush and point out that he had spent all of his school holidays in the place since kindergarten, so he should know the ropes.

Sally and Joel had known each other all their lives; their fathers were golfing buddies and the children all went to the local school together, albeit spread over a few years. That was how she got the job in the first place. Originally it was a work experience placement, as a favour to her father, but she fitted in so well she was offered a full-time job and started on the Monday after she left school.

She and Joel had even dated a few times in high school, but nothing came of it, much to their father's disappointment. Sally could never remember why.

They lost touch when he went away to university and when he came back to the company full time it never really came up. They both dated other people and by the time he took the top job, they had each become engaged. But they were close colleagues and firm friends. So, she felt quite comfortable when he indicated for her to sit on the office couch and then sat down close beside her, handing her a glass of excellent whisky.

He pulled off his fake beard, sipped his drink, and then rested his head back.

"It's good to relax," he said, stretching his arm out along the top of the couch behind Sally's head.

"Is that the same move you used when we went to the movies in school?" she teased.

"Not at all," Joel said with a chuckle. "In school I didn't give you booze first!"

"Maybe that was your mistake," she quipped.

"Maybe," he said with a smile and took another sip.

He didn't move his arm away. It wasn't touching her, and she wasn't uncomfortable. They sat in very companionable silence, drinking and winding down.

"Will you be alone tomorrow Sal?" he asked casually

Sally wasn't sure how to answer. She hadn't told anybody about breaking off her engagement to Damian yet. She was trying to keep it from getting to her parents before they got back. They never would have gone if they had known. But Joel went to the same gym and knew Damian, at least in passing. So, he must have heard.

"Yes," she said after a lengthy pause. "But I'll be fine." Sally wasn't sure even she believed that.

"You should come to the house. It isn't as if we won't have enough to go around and you already know everybody. Both of our parents will skin us alive if they find out you spent Christmas alone when you could have come to be with us for the day."

Sally's first impulse was to decline. She didn't get on well with Joel's fiancé Natalia, but the rest of the family were lovely and what Joel said about their parents was right. So, she considered it, thinking she could suck up her discomfort with Natalia for one day.

As if he could hear Sally's thoughts, Joel said, "She won't be there."

Sally looked at him questioningly.

"Natalia, I mean," he added.

Sally assumed Natalia was away for a modelling assignment and tried not to look relieved. "Yes, thanks Joel, that would be lovely, if you think your parents won't mind,"

"They will love it," he said cheerily.

They fell silent again and Sally had mentally moved on when Joel withdrew his arm from the back of the couch and sat forward as if contemplating his drink. He sat there for long enough for Sally to wonder if he was okay, then he sat back and looked at her.

"Natalia and I have split up." He looked almost relieved to have said it out loud.

"I'm so sorry Joel," she said almost by reflex.

"No need to be, I'm fine. Or at least I will be" Then he paused again and put his arm back up on the couch. "We had an enormous fight after Natalia said it was disgusting how much Angela had let herself go after the last baby."

Sally was confused for a moment. "Angela?" she asked. "Your sister Angela?"

"Yep," he nodded again.

"Natalia said Angela had let herself go?"

Joel nodded and then he sighed. "We then got into a raging fight which ended in her telling me she was never having kids because they ruin a woman's body. I was pretty upset. It all got very ugly and we called it quits." He took a long sip of his drink.

"I'm sorry, Joel. That's awful."

"I'm not sorry," he said. "It was just the last straw, you know? There were other issues." He drained his glass. "Seconds?" he asked as he rose to head for the bar.

"No thanks," Sally said holding up her still half full glass. She watched him walk across his office. He was in his Santa suit but without his beard.

"What are you grinning at?" he asked as he returned

"Just you in your outfit looking like a young sexy Santa," she said.

"Sexy, eh?" he said striking a pose just before he sat back down. "And you can hardly talk, Mrs. Claus. That skirt of yours is nowhere near regulation length."

They both laughed. It was a bit of an inside joke, referring to the high school deputy that was obsessed with the length of the girl's school uniforms and ended up banning 'fraternisation' between male and female students after she caught the school captain sitting on her boyfriend's knee in the library.

"Would you like to sit on Santa's lap and tell him what you want for Christmas?" he said with a wink.

"So, you think that being a single man means you can flirt with all the girls now do you?" she teased.

"Only the pretty ones," he said. Then an odd look came over his face. "Actually, no," he continued in a more serious tone. "Only with you."

Sally suddenly realised he had become serious. She laughed a little uneasily and squirmed under his gaze. Joel leaned forward a little and Sally pulled back.

"Oh, Joel." She tried to sound playful, despite feeling unusually bashful for a moment and hoping he didn't notice "For a minute there it looked like you were going to kiss me."

He didn't respond immediately. Instead, he looked deep into her eyes and she suddenly felt quite naked.

"I think I am going to kiss you, Sally," he said. "Unless you object."

She looked back at him, making sure he wasn't joking and wondering if it would be more awkward in the morning if they crossed that line or if she tried to backtrack now. He was a really nice guy, one of life's real gentlemen, but she still had a moment of fear that things could get difficult at work after this and she loved her job.

She looked at his face; he was lovely, and she knew she cared deeply for him. She realised she did find him very attractive. Either way, it was going to potentially be awkward so she decided to lead with her heart.

"No, Joel," she almost whispered. "I don't object."

The smile on his face was charmingly disarming as he put his hand up to cup her cheek. "Are you sure, Sal? We can stop here, no hard feelings no damage done."

She carefully examined his expression, then closed her eyes briefly as she considered how she was feeling. Her heart was fluttering, whether from nerves or something else she couldn't tell, but she felt safe and a part of her ached to feel his lips on hers. It always had.

She lifted her hand and gently ran one fingertip along his slightly stubbled jaw. "Kiss me please, Joel," she said.

He did. His lips were soft and warm, and his mouth tasted of whiskey and fruitcake. He was gentle, amazingly gentle. She hadn't been kissed like that since…she couldn't remember when, if ever. He cupped her face in his hand and kissed her more deeply but still his tongue was controlled, exploratory but not probing. Gently massaging hers rather than invading her mouth.

His kiss was warm, comfortable, and made Sally feel safe. Even his all-day stubble was just a delicate graze on her soft face. He kissed her neck, his breath cascading gently over her skin. His voice was deep and rich when he whispered in her ear, "God, you're beautiful."

Sally felt her body responding to him, her heart quickened, and she felt her face flushing. She felt his whispering again. "I want you, Sal. I want to make love to you. Are you with me? Is that okay?"

She couldn't remember a guy having asked her so nicely before. Damian certainly never did. It felt a bit alien. Nice, but alien. She was on unfamiliar ground and not sure what to do. She didn't respond at first. Her heart was beating hard and she feared she might break into a sweat, but Joel just waited patiently, and she realised she couldn't resist that.

She kissed him, and his tenderness almost melted her heart. He pulled back enough to look into her eyes and Sally thought she saw a fleeting glimpse of something smouldering deep inside of him before it was replaced with a look of concern.

"Do you want to stop, Sal?" He looked questioningly at her as if trying to read her face. "It's fine if you do. I'm fine. We're fine. We don't have to do this," he said earnestly as he went to move away.

"Don't go, Joel," Sally said. "Please, kiss me some more."

The smile on his face made Sally's heart flutter. His kiss was sensual and warm. It was her turn to draw back and investigate his face for a moment. She studied him, this handsome, kind, gentle man, and she realised she was going to let him go as far as he wanted regardless of the consequences. The look on Joel's face was predominantly calm if a little confused and anxious. She finally put him out of his misery.

"Make love to me," she whispered. "Please, Joel. I want you to."

He grinned broadly and put one finger up as if asking her to wait for a minute. He got up and went into his bathroom. When he came out, he quickly showed her a condom before putting it into his jacket pocket. She almost laughed at the comedy of putting a condom into the pocket of a Santa suit, but she managed to just smile at how cute he looked doing it.

He sat back down beside her and patted his lap. "Come sit on my knee," he quipped with a wink.

Sally chuckled and moved herself to sit across Santa's lap to kiss him. He put his hands gently on the back of her head and ran his fingers carefully through her hair, just below where her hat was. He kissed her mouth deeply, then her ear, whispering, "Thank you," as he moved his tender lips to her neck and throat.

Sally could feel herself growing warm between her legs as Joel ran his hand across her breast, making her nipple start to harden and become visible through her clothes. He undid the buttons at the front of her dress and slid one side off her shoulder. He kissed his way down from her throat to her chest and ran his soft lips across the flesh protruding above the lace of her bra.

She hoped he would notice it was done up at the front and undo it, but he didn't. She was aching to feel his mouth on her breast so much; she had to tell him.

"It undoes at the front," she said and they both seemed to reach for the clasp at the same time leading to an awkward fumbling moment which ended in Sally undoing her own bra. Something she didn't recall ever having to do before. But when he ran his tongue over her nipple and sucked the rock-hard nub into his soft, warm mouth the awkwardness passed.

Sally closed her eyes and felt herself becoming aroused as Joel alternately licked and kissed her breast and flicked her aching nipple with the tip of his tongue. She could feel him growing hard beneath her and that made her so wet, she started to squirm on his lap.

He ran one hand up her thigh, making eye contact as if to check that was okay. She nodded, thinking this was the politest sex she'd ever had. She wondered if this was how other people usually did things and hoped it was just part of a slow build. They moaned quietly, almost in unison, when his hand finally reached the damp crotch of her knickers. He rubbed the fabric around and over her quickly swelling lips until Sally was panting in anticipation of being touched. Then he carefully moved the material to the side and began to play with her soft folds.

Sally was on the verge of begging him to go inside her, but she stayed quiet. Joel kept playing. He licked his fingers and slid the wet tips between her lips, spreading the moisture and teasing them apart just a little. Just enough for him to work his way up to her throbbing clitoris. She sighed, almost with relief, when he finally touched her there and she felt herself beginning to get properly wet.

He smiled and kissed her as he played with her, confidently manipulating her blood-filled nub until she was on the verge of orgasm. Part of her wished he would tease her more, let her build and make her really ache. Another part wanted to beg him not to stop. But she didn't want him to think badly of her, so she just stayed quiet and prayed he would get her off.

Sally didn't have long to wait. Soon enough Joel's seemingly expert fingers had her desperately working to hold back her cries as he pushed her up and over the edge into a lovely climax.

She put her hand down onto his to let him know he could stop, and Joel put his arm around her and drew her to his chest. She rested her head on his shoulder to catch her breath, panting. He turned his head, kissed her nose, and held her tightly to him. She felt warm and safe, but she found herself wondering if he was going to make his move. She could feel how hard he was, so she knew he was turned on, but he seemed content just to hold her.

She knew countless of her friends would give anything to have a man hold them like that after orgasm, but Sally was worried that he didn't want her. She squirmed and became a little restless but was not sure how to bring it up. Finally, she managed to just say it.

"Don't you want me, Joel?"

Joel looked at her, a little startled. "Of course, I want you," he said. "Can't you feel how much I want you?" He moved his hips to accentuate the erection pressing into her buttocks.

"Yes, I can feel it, but you don't seem very... eager," she managed to say but very quietly.

He smiled and kissed her. "I am very eager, believe me, I want you desperately. I just don't want to rush you." He kissed her on the forehead. "But as soon as you feel ready…"

Sally smiled and kissed him. "I'm very, very ready," she said.

Joel stood them both up and undid the drawstring on his costume. His pants fell to the floor and he stepped out of them before sitting back down. She could see his hard-on bulging in his underwear and she ached to have it in her mouth, but it seemed she wasn't going to have that opportunity. He released it from his boxers and before Sally had even had much of a chance to admire its rigid form, he was rolling a condom down over it. Then he put his arms out to encourage her to straddle his lap.

She did so eagerly. Joel reached down between her legs. This was all new to Sally and she felt a little lost. She was expecting a bit more play, but he slid her underwear to the side and moved her closer to him. He pressed the head of his erection against her soft lips, sliding it back and forth to get it wet. Then he held himself at her opening and said, "Slide down on me, beautiful."

Sally wasn't really used to being on top, or having much control, so she found it a bit confronting, but she put her hands on his shoulders and pressed herself down onto him, engulfing him completely. Feeling his hardness deep inside her made her moan quietly. He felt really good in her. He was a bit bigger than she was used to, so he filled and stretched her just a little. She wished he would grab her and take her, but he moved his hands to her buttocks, holding her knickers to one side with his fingertips, then smiled at her kindly.

"You lead, beautiful. Take it the way you like it."

Sally was not sure what to do really. She wasn't used to being in charge. She knew he was actually being considerate, but it made her feel like he didn't really want her. She rocked back and forth on him, feeling him deep in her, then she started to slide up and down on him, trying to take him the way she thought she should. He started to meet her movements with thrusts of his own until they found a good rhythm. Sally relaxed into it and decided being on top wasn't so bad...in fact, it was pretty good.

She looked into Joel's face and could see tremendous concentration, like he was doing his utmost to maintain some control of himself and she suddenly realised he must be trying not to orgasm too soon. She slowed down a little so as to not embarrass him. Not that she minded; she doubted she was going to orgasm again, not like this.

They moved together, Joel pulling Sally closer to kiss her as she could feel him building to a climax. She could see the effort of his self-control beading on his skin and she decided to put him out of his misery. She rode him as hard and as fast as she dared without risking Joel thinking she was some sort of slut and before very long he threw his head back and groaned his way through his orgasm.

He pulled her close, panting, and held her until he caught his breath. Then he kissed her and lifted her off him, excusing himself to go to the bathroom. Presumably, to take care of the condom, Sally thought. When he came back, she excused herself and went to the loo to tidy herself up a bit.

When she returned, she felt a little awkward until he smiled at her and patted his lap. She sat across him again and let him hold her. It was really very nice. He was a truly nice guy, she was just used to things being rougher. But you can't have it both ways I guess, she thought to herself.

After a long silence Joel said, "Do you think we could give it another try Sal? Dating, I mean."

Sally didn't respond for a while. She was considering her feelings. She was a bit confused as to why she didn't just say yes! He was a great guy, everything about him was fabulous. Joel was kind, considerate, good looking, smart, had a great family, her parents already liked him and so did she.

So, what if the sex was a bit dull? she thought. But she wasn't sure if she was ready to settle for 'comfortable sex' just yet. Then she remembered her cousin once warning her not to marry a pig just because he was good in bed. "Sooner or later he will be out fucking around while you need him to be home putting the bins out and helping bathe the kids."

Sally realised she could rely on Joel to be there for kids and bins; besides he was only asking her to date. She could change her mind and she guessed she could find another job if she needed to. Much as she would hate that. It occurred to her that she had been silent quite a while and that Joel was waiting patiently for her reply. How could she forgo a man like that just because the sex didn't set her on fire?

She looked up into his eyes to speak, but he beat her to it.

"I'm sorry, Sal. I shouldn't have asked. It was wrong, and you don't have to say anything. We're all good. Truly."

Sally put her fingertip against his lips to shush him. Then she smiled and said, "I'd like it if we had another go at dating. Just so long as the boss is okay with fraternisation amongst the staff."

The grin that spread across Joel's face could have outshone all the fairy lights in the whole city. "Do you mean it?" he asked like a big foolish kid. "I didn't mean to pressure you."

"Will you please take 'yes' for an answer?" Sally said and kissed him.

He pulled back smiling and said, "I'll clear it with the boss." Then they kissed again before Joel put his arm around her and drew her close. She rested her head on his shoulder, and it occurred to her that they had made love without their hats even falling off. She was happy with the notion of dating such a nice guy and even let herself imagine the possibility of more of a future together. But the prospect of a life of lukewarm sex was a bit of a cloud over her parade. She sighed.

"That's a big sigh, baby," Joel said. "Are you okay?"

"I'm fine," Sally lied...well it wasn't really a lie, she thought. It was a half-truth. She was fine and she would be fine, it was just a bit of an adjustment. Not that sex with Damian was ever great - far from it...but it was always hot. But he was wrong for her in so many other ways and if she had to choose between a life of hot sex with a pig and a life of warm and comfortable sex with an otherwise perfect guy; the choice was easy, really. And it might not even be a lifetime. Dating didn't work for them last time, but she could never remember why.

"Sal." Joel's voice broke through her introspection. She looked up at him. "It didn't rock your world, did it baby?" he said.

The ease at which he had taken to calling her baby felt really nice, and she was still half in her daydream state, so she answered without really thinking. "Umm not really," she confessed. "But it was nice," she added hastily when she realised she had said that out loud.

"Nice?" he repeated and mimed an arrow to the heart "Ouch," he added.

"I'm sorry, I didn't mean.... I ... just oh, I didn't... and you caught me off guard....and I..." Sally stammered incoherently.

Joel put his finger to her lips and laughed. Sally laughed too and slapped him gently on the shoulder. "Meanie," she said

Once they settled, he said, "Seriously baby, I'm not so insensitive that I can't see that didn't do it for you."

Sally went to speak but Joel shushed her and kissed her then held her to his chest. She felt like crying. She didn't want to mess this up before they went anywhere at all. "I'm sorry," she said quietly "Don't be upset with me, please."

He kissed her on the head. "I'm not upset with you, Sal. Not at all." Then there was a long silence before Joel spoke again. "So, despite the sex being just 'nice' you still want to give dating another go?"

Sally could only nod. She felt awful about the 'nice' comment.

Joel kissed her head and fell silent again for a while. "May I ask a personal question?" he said

"Sure," Sally managed, still feeling like a heel.

"Why did you break up with Damian?"

"Lots of reasons," Sally said, then realised that was a pretty poor answer. "He was too unreliable and indiscrete mostly."

"Not because he was too... rough?" Joel ventured

"Well, yes, he was too rough in a lot of ways and often rude to my parents."

"But I mean rough as in...was he too rough in bed?" Joel clarified.

"Oh that, no, not at all. That wasn't a problem," Sally said, wondering if she should have said that out loud.

"So, he wasn't too rough for you?"

Sally sat up and looked at Joel. He clearly wanted to know something specific, and she wasn't giving him the information he wanted.

"What are you asking me, Joel?" she said straight up, feeling a little frustrated. "I'll tell you whatever you want to know but I don't know what you want."

"I know Damian," he said. "And I know what he is like with women and I am wondering if he was too rough for you in bed or if you liked it like that?"

Sally felt herself blush. She didn't answer for a moment. She wasn't sure what to say. There was no sign of judgement in Joel's voice, but she was still very unsure. He spoke again before she did. "There is no danger in being honest with me, Sal. I'm asking because I need to know." She decided honesty was the best idea. She took a deep breath and steadied herself.

"Damian was not too rough for me." She looked down because it was too hard to look at Joel. She feared seeing the judgment in his eyes "In fact, I would sometimes have liked him to be rougher if I thought I could trust him to stay in control and if I wasn't worried what he would tell his friends or say in front of my family. There is a lot more I would have liked him to do, if not for that." There was silence and Sally felt quite exposed and totally humiliated "Please don't hate me, Joel. You did ask, I'm just..."

She didn't get to finish what she was saying. Joel kissed her - really kissed her. He held her head firmly in his hands, his mouth pressed hard against hers. His stubble rasped her face and lips as his tongue pressed and probed her mouth, invading her, possessing her, making her ache.

He grabbed her hair in his fist and pulled her head to the side. He ran his tongue up her neck to her ear and practically growled. "Let's try again shall we, Princess? Only this time I'll show you how I like it." He bit her earlobe, hard enough to make her almost cry. "Do you have a safe word little one?" he asked.

His voice, his words, and the whole change of energy were sending a pulsing thrill through her as she shook her head...not trusting herself to speak.

Joel loosened his grip on Sally's hair, just a little, and looked around him, searching for a suitable word it seemed. He kept shaking his head almost imperceptibly, obviously dismissing some. Then he grinned broadly and said in an amused voice, "Okay, Princess. For tonight at least, your safe word is Christmas. Say it once if I am getting a bit too close to the edge for you, but twice will stop me dead and we'll re-assess. Can you remember that?"

Sally nodded.

"Good girl," Joel said. "Now let's have some fun."

He tightened his grip on her hair again, picked her up in his arms, and carried her across the office. He stood her up and leant her backside against his desk. Sally was panting, her heart beating loudly in her ears. She felt confused, unsure of what was happening, but arousal was flooding through her and she was sure she didn't want it to stop.

"Are you wearing anything important to you?" he demanded.

"Only my jewellery," she responded.

"Good," he said, and then he gripped the front of her dress in both hands and tore it open. Sally gasped as he ripped the top of the dress off her completely. It took him less than a second to unclip what had earlier seemed tricky and then throw the bra on the floor. Her nipples were instantly hard and aching, and her body was flooded with adrenalin and began to tremble.

She felt Joel's hot gaze on her naked breasts and saw him grin before he grabbed one roughly in his strong hand and squeezed it, sucking the nipple hard into his mouth. Sally moaned and felt her wetness surging between her thighs and saturating her knickers.

Joel kept a firm grip on Sally's hair and continued to kiss and bite her breasts, chest, and neck as he put his hand under what was left of her skirt. Without hesitation, he slid his fingers under the elastic of her underwear and ran the tips along her lips.

He groaned as he felt just how wet she was. "You really do like it like this don't you, baby?" he all but growled in her ear. "Feel how wet you are."

He pushed her harder against his desk and slid a finger deep up inside her.

"Yes," she moaned without thinking.

That seemed to encourage him. He kissed her hard and as his tongue wrestled hers, he pushed another finger hard up into her, making her squeal into his mouth. He groaned and pushed up into her harder, sliding his fingers out and then plunging them back into her. She could feel her juices running down her thigh as his stubble stung her chin.

Without warning, he let go of her hair and pushed her back onto the clean mahogany surface of his desk.

"Spread your legs," he demanded.

Sally complied, and he pulled the soaking wet knickers to the side to push his fingers hard into her, rubbing her G-spot with more pressure than she had ever felt before. He placed the palm of his other hand on her mound and pressed down on her lower belly with his fingers. The sensation of what his fingers were doing inside of her increased and she began to moan loudly. She had never felt pleasure so intense until Joel slid his thumb over her swollen, aching clit.

Sally instantly exploded into an orgasm with no warning.

"Good girl," Joel growled.

Sally laid panting on the desk, thinking she had died and gone to heaven. Joel winked at her.

"Better than 'nice'?" he asked in a cocky tone.

All she could do was grin and nod.

Then he bent down and took the waistband of her knickers in his teeth and pulled with his hands, tearing them completely in half. Before Sally even had time to respond he had pushed her legs up, spread them wide apart, and his tongue was deep up inside her. She squealed and squirmed under his mouth as he licked and sucked her, loudly lapping up her wetness and occasionally using the tip of his tongue to flick her still sensitive clit.

Once she could stand the flicks without squirming too much, Joel pressed his fingers up into her again and worked on her clit in earnest with his lips and tongue. Sally could feel the orgasm building this time but as she reached the point of no return, Joel dragged his stubbled jaw across the tip of her throbbing mound and sent her skyrocketing into a whole new experience. She squealed as wave after wave of pleasure shot through her like an electric current.

Once again, she found herself panting on Joel's desk. This time she could feel the puddle forming underneath her. She tried to speak but it was too much effort. Joel let her catch her breath before he pulled the hair on her mound with his teeth. He pulled so hard it made her eyes water and then bit her all the way up her belly, leaving a trail of red marks.

He moved around to the side of the desk and took both of Sally's wrists in one hand, pinning them above her head. She squirmed against him. Not because she wanted him to release her but because she wanted to feel his strength, his power to hold her, and the struggle felt delicious. He reached down and began to finger her again. Only so much rougher than he had before. Rougher than Damian ever had. Rougher than anybody ever had. She could hear how wet she was from the noise it made each time Joel plunged into her.

"You are so fucking wet baby," he said. "And you taste as hot as fuck. Here taste yourself." He slid his fingers out of her pussy and put them towards her mouth. She had never had her own juices in her mouth and her first response was to turn her head away. But Joel just laughed at her, grabbed her chin, and smeared her juices all over her closed mouth. Then he leant forward to kiss her with her juices still all over his face.

He forced his tongue into her mouth and made her taste her own musky bitterness and as he did, she could feel herself flooding the desk. He pulled back and looked into her eyes. "You have the power to stop me you know. Remember that, Princess. But trust me, you will learn to love how you taste as much as I do." He put his finger back inside her and then back to her mouth. She pulled away again. She didn't want him to stop; she wanted him to force her. The feeling of struggling against him, of resisting him, was making her hotter than she could ever have imagined.

Joel laughed again and she knew he was enjoying the game too. He kept smearing her juices all over her mouth and face, then finally he grabbed her jaw hard and pulled it down to force two fingers into her mouth.

"Suck them," he demanded in a tone that almost made Sally orgasm again just on its own. She sucked his fingers. Two at first, then he put three, then four. Her mouth was stuffed full, and she couldn't swallow. He drew them out and kissed her hard.

"Good girl," he said. "You look good with pussy juice all over your face." He ran his tongue across her lips. "Mmmm. You taste good too. You will come to love that, Princess. I promise you that." The idea that he intended for them to do this again sent a searing bolt of pleasure up Sally's spine and right into her brain as if branding it.

He stood her up and made her bend over the desk. Her mind was racing with possibilities, and her blood was surging through her like never before. He lifted what was left of her skirt up over her hips, exposing her naked buttocks, causing another rush of adrenalin. She felt so exposed, so controlled by Joel's demanding passion, and at the same time being on display like that was making her feel deliciously vulnerable.

He was obviously examining her. She could feel his burning gaze on her skin and it made her ache. He ran his hands over her cheeks, squeezing them, parting them, kneading them.

Then without warning, Joel landed a hard-stinging slap across one cheek.

Sally squealed but the sting quickly gave way to a spreading warmth. The second slap stung more. But it melted into a warm glow rapidly, too. By the time the fourth one landed she had tears running down her face and was just about to use her safe word when she felt Joel's warm lips on her burning flesh, and it felt so good it was worth it.

Joel kissed his way up her back to her shoulders and whispered in her ear, "You were a perfect brave girl, and I'm proud of you." Then he put his hand between her legs and said "See how wet you are, Princess? See how much you liked that?" He kissed her neck and shoulders while he played almost absentmindedly with her wet lips until her tears stopped and the glow from her buttocks was spreading over her body.

She began to move and press against Joel's hand, letting herself get lost in the sensation of his touch. She was so turned on and felt so good she could have stayed there forever.

"You like that don't you, Princess?" Joel purred in her ear.

She nodded.

"My naughty hot girl." He chuckled. "You think that is the end, but it is just the beginning. Now I'm going to fuck you like the dirty bitch you want to be."

Sally shuddered.

He left her face down on the desk and moved to stand behind her. He paused for a moment and she assumed it was for a condom, but she couldn't see him.

"Spread your legs for me," he commanded. Sally spread her legs and could feel her juices running freely down her thighs, soaking the tops of her long red socks. She felt the smooth hard head of Joel's cock sliding around in her juices, getting nice and slick. When he pushed himself into her, she groaned with deep pleasure. He grabbed her hips hard and pulled her towards him. She was full, so full of him, and she never wanted to be any other way.

Her mind was a whirl of lust and she didn't think she ever imagined sex could be this good. She couldn't believe this was the same man she had been disappointed with just a little while ago. How could this hot, wild, powerful man have been so polite and demure? How could she not have seen this in him? Then she realised she had seen it. The straining to control himself, the tiny beads of sweat had nothing to do with trying not to cum too soon. They were from the effort it took to keep his passion under control.

She felt his rigid cock moving slowly in and out of her but soon the thrusts became hard and rough. Sometimes he pulled right out of her then slammed himself back in. She was so wet and so turned on he slipped into her easily despite his size, and each thrust filled her and made her groan. His hands were spread across her rear end, squeezing and kneading.

"You look so good with my cock in you, Princess, and your cheeks are so pretty and red." He pulled her cheeks apart. "And look at that pretty arsehole." He rubbed a wet thumb over the tender puckered flesh. Sally felt a surge of panic run through her. Nobody had ever touched her there. She couldn't believe how good it felt, but she was afraid of what Joel might have in mind. But as if he felt her tension, he said, "Relax, Princess. We will get to that another day."

He moved his hands to her hips and grabbed her with such a strong grip she knew it would bruise. Soon he was pounding into her like a steam train piston. Powerfully, relentlessly, mercilessly, and she loved it. She found herself groaning loudly and felt as if she could almost climax. She had never managed to orgasm like that, but she felt like she could now.

Joel grabbed her hips. "Tilt" he commanded and she angled her hips the way he pushed her.

"Fuck," she cried out unexpectedly as her pleasure skyrocketed. The head of his cock was now hitting her somewhere; she couldn't tell where, just somewhere magical and each thrust sent such a bolt of ecstasy through her.

"Say it again, baby," Joel said. "I want to hear it."

She felt lost in some other reality but could soon hear herself repeating "Fuck... fuck...fuck," each time Joel hit the spot, and soon she was certain she could orgasm like that. But each time she thought she was close, Joel backed off and after a while, she was ready to beg for release, but she struggled to speak.

Just as she began to wonder if it would ever end and if Joel would ever let her cum, she heard herself cry out as she arched her back and found herself riding a wave of throbbing pleasure that went on and on. Before she really had time to recover she found herself dragged off the desk and onto her knees in front of Joel, confronted by his enormous hard-on.

Without thinking she ripped the condom off him and plunged him into her mouth. She had always enjoyed the feeling of a smooth hard cock in her mouth and Joel's felt like perfection as she rolled her tongue over the tip and around the edges, seeking out his special spots.

"Time for exploring later," he said as he ripped the hat off her head and grabbed two handfuls of hair. He held her head still and fucked her face, hard, rough, making her gag at times. Sally loved it. She licked and slurped as much of him as she could as he rammed his cock into her mouth. She felt tears running down her face and her juices running down her legs and realised she had gone from respectable assistant to hot, wet, slutty mess at the hands of this amazing man.

A tiny part of her brain wanted to worry about the consequences and how this would affect her job, but she was so turned on and Joel was fucking her mouth so perfectly that soon those thoughts were pounded into silence. She put her hands up to feel his butt. She rested her palms on his hard-muscled cheeks and moaned at how good he felt.

Sally ached for Joel to cum in her mouth. She wanted to taste him, she wanted to swallow him. She had never swallowed a man before, but she ached to swallow Joel. But he pulled her up by the hair and stood her up. He reached into his pocket, pulled out another condom, and rolled it over his cock in no time.

Without a word, he pushed Sally until she was lying on her back on the desk and thrust himself into her without preamble. He leant over and bit her shoulder hard enough to make her scream. "I know you wanted me to cum in your mouth, Princess, but I want to cum in your hot sweet cunt tonight. Not until I have fucked you into a quivering mess though."

Sally shuddered; she wasn't sure how much more she could handle. She had never been pushed so far before.

Joel grabbed her legs and forced them apart, holding her thighs in his hands while he fucked her hard and fast. She felt him change position slightly and suddenly he was hitting that magic spot again and soon she was in that whirl of mind-blowing pleasure again screaming, "Fuck, yes fuck me. More, Joel, harder."

She felt rather than heard him order her to tug her nipples. She found it hard to move, but the stern, commanding voice cut through her fog "Now, Princess. Tug your nipples."

She managed to comply.

"Harder, tug them harder," Joel commanded, and soon Sally was pulling and tugging at her nipples so hard she was almost in tears. The tremendous pleasure outweighed the pain and she felt like she was building to an enormous climax that was just barely eluding her.

"Cum for me baby. Cum for me, Princess." She could hear Joel's words, but they didn't make a lot of sense. He was pounding her, and she was tugging her nipples, and she felt like she was racing headlong for a cliff edge. She was crying and trembling all over.

Whimpering her need to the heavens. Then Joel moved his hand and pinched her slippery throbbing clit between his thumb and fingers and jerked it like a tiny cock until she finally arched her back and screamed as she was taken by a mind-fucking monster orgasm and went sailing right over the edge and took flight.

Joel let go of her clit and pressed his body down on to hers but didn't stop fucking her. She didn't care, he could do as he pleased. He had sated her entirely and she now existed merely for him to use for his pleasure. She could feel his searing breath on her neck as he fucked her like a grunting animal.

"I can't wait to fuck your cunt bareback and make you scream," he growled. "I want to watch my cum dripping out of you like a dirty whore. I want to taste it, taste your freshly fucked cunt. I want to make you taste it. I want to do filthy things to you. I want your cunt, I want your mouth, I want your arse. I want to cover every bit of you in cum and make you my filthy dirty slut."

As he spoke, Sally could feel his passion rising, and she knew he was going to cum soon.

"Yes Joel, yes. Fuck me, take me, make me yours. I'll be your dirty slut, baby. I'll let you do anything to me and I'll beg for more. I want your cum in me, I want it in my mouth, in my cunt and yes, Joel I want you to blow your hot cum up my arse."

Joel was fucking her like a beast, grunting and groaning and sweating like an animal. He screamed into her neck as he unloaded his hot cum in wave after wave of groaning, sweating ecstasy. "Fuck, oh fuck, oh fuck," he panted as he collapsed his full weight down on top of Sally struggling to catch his breath.

He moved off her and fumbled around with the condom. Then laid back down beside her. "I'll be glad when we can do without those," he said and kissed her on the cheek.

Sally smiled at the indication that he might want to do it again and that he wanted to be monogamous enough to do without condoms. But her heart crashed when the next thing Joel said was, "I think we should forget about dating, Sal."

She was dumbfounded. She couldn't believe what she was hearing. She suddenly felt very afraid of how this was going to impact on their working relationship. She didn't think she could face him again after this. She wasn't sure she could even face Christmas with his family knowing that he had just fucked her like that and now didn't even want to date.

She was confused and frightened and began to cry.

"Shush now baby," Joel said concerned. "It's all okay. I'm sorry, Sally. You should have stopped me if I was hurting you."

She couldn't tell him what the problem was. Even if she could speak, she didn't think she could articulate her jumbled thoughts.

"Let's get you more comfortable," he said. He got off the desk, pulled off her boots, and carried her to the couch. He sat down and held her in his arms, rocking and soothing her while she cried. She wasn't even sure if she should just get up and leave but he was being so kind while she felt so vulnerable and weak. She didn't want to be alone. So, even though she wanted to slap him and run, she let him hold her and she wept herself to sleep.

When Sally opened her eyes, it took her a while to work out where she was. Then she remembered. She looked around and saw she was lying on Joel's office couch, in his arms with a blanket pulled over the two of them. She tried to peek under the blanket but couldn't see much, so she had a careful feel around. It appeared that they were both naked. She must have really crashed because she had no recollection of taking her socks off or Joel getting the blanket.

Joel stirred. "Good morning sleeping beauty," he said with such a beautiful smile she could almost forget how awful he made her feel.

"Good morning," she said and felt herself blush bright red. The urge to run almost overtook her. The idea that Joel now thought of her as some cheap fuck was almost too much to bear. But it was barely dawn and she was naked. She decided to get out as soon as she could, go home, and start looking for another job as soon as Christmas was over. She really didn't think she could face him every day now.

"Would you like to shower?" he asked. She was suddenly very pleased she had talked his father into putting in a full bathroom for when he pulled all-nighters.

"Yes, thanks," she said and tried to get up and walk to the bathroom with as much dignity as she could muster.

The hot water felt fantastic and she was determined not to cry. She wished she had thought to bring her clothes in with her, but it was too late for that. At least she'd have a towel to cover herself with, and once she got out of there, she could put all the embarrassment behind her. She thought she was beginning to feel a bit better, or a bit cleaner at any rate, when she heard Joel's voice. "Mind if I join you?" he said.

Part of her wanted to tell him to get lost, but she couldn't bring herself to. He was naked and smiling and looking so good. She hadn't really had the chance to admire his body before. He was lean and fit and perfectly muscled. She wondered how she had not noticed his abs the night before. They looked so delicious she wanted to run her hands all over them. Then she looked a bit lower and remembered that she had been preoccupied with other parts of him the night before.

"Sal?" he said. "May I join you?" His voice brought her back from her daydream and she felt no ability to resist.

"Sure," she said.

As soon as he got in, he took her in his arms and kissed her. She was becoming more confused by the moment. She pulled away and found the courage to say, "I don't think we should, Joel."

He wasn't put off at all. He just smiled dazzlingly and said, "I know Santa is only meant to come once a year baby, but I didn't think that was about what he did with Mrs. Claus."

Sally's head was awash with desire and confusion. She thought she should also be feeling regret. But she wasn't. She felt quite comfortable here in the shower with her naked boss. She couldn't make head nor tail of it. She finally plucked up the courage to say, "But Joel, we are not Mr. and Mrs. Claus. And you said you don't even want us to give dating a go again. So maybe we should just... not." Despite her best efforts not to cry, she could feel tears rolling down her cheeks.

"Oh," he said, looking chastened as the penny suddenly dropped. "Oh shit," he said. "I'm sorry, baby, I thought the tears were because I hurt you."

"You did hurt me," Sally blurted out. "Fucking a girl like that and then saying you don't even want to date her is pretty hurtful you know." Then she slapped his chest and his shoulder and said, "I should hate you for that." She kept slapping him.

"Woah, woah, woah girl," Joel said and took hold of both her wrists. "Settle baby, before somebody gets hurt."

"I'm already hurt!" she screamed at him. She hadn't realised just how upset she was until that moment. Then she burst into tears and all but collapsed into his arms. "I was okay until you made me tell you I like it rough and fucked me like an animal. You made it so that nobody is ever going to be good enough again. And now I have to go home to an empty house and find a new job. And you want to play Mr. and Mrs. Clause with me when you don't even want to date me!" Sally ranted.

Joel pulled her close. "I'm sorry baby. So sorry. I had no idea. You had just rocked my whole world and I was clumsy. I'm so sorry, please forgive me. Settle please, little one. Hush now and let me explain."

Sally let him hold her and let the tears run down her cheeks as the warm water flowed over her back.

"I'm sorry, Sally. You don't need to go home to an empty house." She went to object and he shushed her.

"Let me speak baby," he said in a firm but kind tone. "You do not have to go home to an empty house, you do not even have to go home at all if you don't want to, and you don't need a new job. I couldn't manage without you and when I said we should forget about dating what I was trying to say was…will you marry me, Sally? Please Sally, please forgive last night's clumsy just fucked attempt at a proposal and please marry me."

Sally wasn't sure she was hearing correctly "Pardon?" she said

Joel got down on one knee in the shower with the water running over him and tried to speak but he was having so much trouble Sally stepped to the side to block the water from hitting his face.

"Marry me, Sally," he said. "I don't want to date you, I want you to be my wife, and I want that as soon as possible before you have the chance to get away. I have never met a girl like you. You are perfection. I always thought I had to choose between a girl I wanted in bed and a girl I wanted out of bed. But baby, with you I can fuck you senseless and then take you home to my parents. You are everything I need, and I want to be your husband."

Sally was stunned…relieved but stunned. She needed to absorb it all. She knew what she was going to say, but she didn't want to rush it.

"I'll need to think about it, Joel," she said. After a moment a sly grin spread over her face. "But while your down there."

Joel grinned and put his hands on her hips, pinning her to the wall. He lifted one of her legs up over his shoulder and plunged his tongue deep into her without hesitation. Sally moaned and gripped his hair for support. Joel licked her and bit her and tongue fucked her to two amazing orgasms. Then he stood up and kissed her. He had been right, she was already enjoying the taste of her wetness on his mouth, but there was still something she wanted to taste before she gave him her response.

"There is something I need to check first," she said when he looked to her for an answer.

She slid down on to her knees and took Joel's cock into her mouth. She moaned at the way it felt on her tongue. She smiled at the way he moaned as she explored and teased and learned all his secret, sensitive spots. She cupped his balls in her hand and explored them in ways she had never been able to do before. He seemed content to let her explore and play, but she wanted to taste him, wanted to feel him cum in her mouth. She looked up at him and smiled.

"Fuck my mouth please, Joel."

He smiled down at her and said: "With pleasure, baby."

He held her head still and fucked her mouth hard and fast. Sally loved the way his fists felt in her hair. The feeling of his cock pounding on the back of her throat made her pussy wet as she concentrated on trying not to gag too much. Before long, she could feel Joel was getting close. She put her hands on his backside to show she wanted it in her mouth. But as he began to twitch and groan and she could feel him beginning to fill her mouth he pulled her head back off his cock. "You can't have it all baby, I want to see some on your face." She swallowed what she could and felt the warm spray of the rest of it on her face and chest.

Joel groaned as he squeezed the last of his cum out onto Sally's body and stood over her in a way to prevent the shower washing it straight off. Sally took stock of her situation. She was kneeling in front of the now flaccid cock of the most amazing man she had ever known, with his hot cum all over her face and tits and the taste of him still in her mouth, and he was waiting for her to give him an answer to his proposal of marriage. She giggled.

"What's so funny, beautiful?" he asked.

She didn't answer him. She just took his hands and let him help her up. She pressed her messy body against him and kissed him deeply. He was not phased by that at all. She rested her head on his strong chest and he automatically put his arms around her.

She looked up at him and said, "Yes, Joel, I'll marry you."

His grin could have lit up the sky. He kissed her for an age then cleaned her off and got her out heading as if to get dressed but Sally said, "Where do you keep the condoms baby?"

Joel pointed to the draw and Sally reached in for one.

"Now what were you saying about fucking me senseless before taking me home to your parents?"

Joel laughed, picked her up and threw her over his shoulder. She giggled and struggled all the way to the couch. They fucked like wild animals all morning until they were both totally spent. Then they laid on the couch in each other's arms, safe and content.

Sally looked up at Joel and said, "I think I love you, Mr. Claus."

"I've always loved you, Mrs. Claus," he said and smiled the smile of a happy boy that had got all that he ever wanted for Christmas.

*****

The Naughty List

"**B**endryn Elford! Where the devil is my naughty list?" Santa's bellow was so loud it rattled the whole workshop and sent the maintenance elves into a flurry of activity, grabbing their brooms and shovels to clean up the piles of snow that sloughed off the roof.

"Bendryn!" Santa shouted again, but there was no answer.

Bendryn had taken off and was running as fast as his legs could carry him to where he had left Rudolph, just outside the gate with a bag of oats.

He knew Santa could simply bring them back in an instant, with a wave of his hand, as soon as he realised they had pulled an Elvis and left the building. But Bendryn was hoping they could make it to the time-slip before that happened. That way, he may get some hours in normal earth time to explore the naughty list better before they got dragged back.

He could hear Santa bellowing in the distance as he leapt on to Rudolph's back and said, "Now big fella, as fast as you can, or we'll have no fun before we get recalled."

Rudolph sprang into action and galloped at breakneck speed straight toward what looked like a solid wall of ice. Just before they hit the wall, Bendryn shut his eyes tight; he hated the next bit. The nimble reindeer did a quick jump to the left, followed by a step to the right and then launched himself straight off a cliff and down into a deep ravine that marked the space between Christmas time and normal time before finally taking flight towards the prearranged coordinates: Sydney, Australia.

He had decided on Australia because it was summer there, which might make it easier to find somebody willing to take their clothes off. Or so he hoped.

They were safe for a while now. They were travelling in space but not time, so it didn't matter how long they were in this part of the journey because it took no 'real' time at all. Bendryn had no idea how it worked. All this time and space stuff was too hard for him to grasp. Somebody had tried to explain it to him once and he had a vague idea that it had something to do with a police box, a wardrobe, and lions. But he hadn't really paid any attention. Workshop elves were not meant to leave the North Pole alone, so he didn't really need to understand the intricacies of such things.

He just needed to know how to make toys. He was a fiftieth-generation toymaker and so that was all that was expected of him. But now that he had turned eighty-five and Santa had announced his impending promotion, he was determined to have some fun before he was tied down to his adult duties. The idea of taking on his role as Third Assistant Sub-Apprentice to the Second Vice-Head of Painting and Construction before he'd even kissed a girl was just too depressing.

So, he had decided to get hold of the naughty list, grab himself a reindeer, and take himself off on an elven version of rumspringa before he settled down. After all, he figured, if it was good enough for the Amish why wouldn't it be good enough for the elvish?

He didn't allow himself to think of the consequences. He had no idea what Santa would do when he got back. He had never known an elf to do such a thing before, unless you count his fourteenth cousin, Heldryn Elford. He had run away to New Zealand to try out for a part in a big movie, only to find that fictional elves are much taller and more slender than real elves. He ended up being cast as a smaller, hairy-footed creature in a group scene that ended up on the cutting room floor. The shame was too much for him, and he never came home.

Bendryn felt for the naughty list just to make sure it was still in his pocket. It was a fascinating piece of equipment. It looked like a very ornate scroll that should only open to about arm's length and yet it held the name of everybody that had ever been naughty, as well as details of the naughtiness.

Often the details were quite salacious if you knew where and how to look. It was thought controlled, so you needed to mentally ask the list a question and then know how to see the answer. It could be a bit like looking into a fairground mirror at first, but with a bit of practice Bendryn had worked out how to make it give up its naughtiest secrets.

He was hoping to use it to at least get his first kiss. Although deep down he was hoping for a bit more than that.

He was sure he felt Rudolph chuckle beneath him. Bendryn had long suspected that reindeer were telepathic, but they always denied it. 'They would' he thought and was sure he felt another suppressed snigger, just as Rudolph changed direction and seemed to be heading straight for the ground at full reindeer speed.

Bendryn shut his eyes and had to bite his knuckle to stop himself from screaming. When he felt it was safe to look, they were on the ground outside their first stop and Rudolph was nibbling on somebody's lawn.

Bendryn checked the list just to make sure they were in the right place. He went to the first address, but nobody was home. The second address was not much better; the girl he was looking for was home but so was her boyfriend. At the third address an enormous angry man wouldn't let him in, and the fourth girl just laughed at him when he explained why he was there. The fifth girl slapped his face and slammed the door.

He finally decided to stop after the sixth girl had looked him up and down, checking out his green tights, green tunic, and matching hat and boots and said: "You think I'd do THAT with a leprechaun?"

He sat on the gutter watching Rudolph nibbling on a neat box hedge and wondered what he was going to do. It had never occurred to him that he couldn't just walk up to a naughty girl and ask for what he wanted. At this rate, Santa would call him back before he had any fun at all. He slumped. 'It's not easy having a good time,' he thought and began to wallow in some serious elf-pity when Rudolph nudged him and Bendryn suddenly thought he needed to change tack.

He opened the naughty list to his full arm's length and thought hard about what he wanted. He could feel the list resisting him, but he focused with all his might and soon a picture started to form of a place called 'The Oxford Tavern.' It was covered in warning stickers that obscured the vision, saying it was a den of iniquity and only very naughty people went there. As Bendryn tilted the list so as to see around the stickers and get a clearer look at the salacious bits, the whole list burst into flames and disintegrated on the spot.

Bendryn and Rudolph were startled by the spontaneous combustion and suddenly wondered how they were going to explain that to Santa when they got back.

"I hope he had that backed up," Bendryn said.

Rudolph shuddered.

After a moment's contemplation Bendryn said, "I think we should push on. If we go home now, we are going to be in trouble anyway and may be grounded for the rest of our lives, so I think we should at least try to have some fun first. Do you think you can find this Tavern?"

Rudolph nodded. Bendryn climbed on and the reindeer leapt into the sky. They had barely reached cruising height when they made a rapid descent and landed in front of a large building on the outskirts of town. Bendryn was not sure which town, he hadn't paid attention in geography either, but it looked like the outskirts of some town or another.

There was a flashing neon sign on the front of the building that alternated between 'The Oxford Tavern' and 'Live Jelly Wrestling.'

Bendryn had no idea why anybody would want to wrestle live jelly. He wasn't sure he even wanted to meet live jelly, but they headed to the door anyway. They were met at the door by an enormous bald man with multiple tattoos on his bare arms.

"You can't bring your goat in here, Robin Hood." He grinned a little menacingly, baring his teeth - all three of them.

"He isn't a goat, he's a deer. And I can't leave him out here. It might not be safe."

Rudolph glared at the big man, who just laughed as he waved them in, "What makes you think he will be any safer inside?"

They walked in and found themselves in a noisy, crowded bar.

The barmaid eyed them up and down then looked admiringly at Rudolph's antlers. "Where were you when we were decorating?" she asked with a chuckle. "What will you have?"

"Two lemonades please," Bendryn replied loudly to be heard over the noise.

The whole room fell silent and the barmaid looked Bendryn and Rudolph up and down again before she asked, "Do we look like the sort of place that serves lemonade to little green men?"

The elf started to quiver out of fear for their safety. The barmaid, whose name tag said Petunia, was a formidable looking woman but Rudolph glared back at her and she seemed to settle all of a sudden and said, "How about a compromise? I can go as far as a shandy."

Bendryn figured the only sensible answer was, "Yes, please, that would be fine. With two straws and a packet of crisps please."

The rest of the patrons seemed to lose interest in the elf and his companion as Bendryn fumbled in his coin purse and came up with some odd coins cousin Heldryn had sent him that were covered in just enough elven magic to prevent Petunia noticing it was the wrong currency. Then they found a table and settled there to have their drinks beside what turned out to be an inflatable swimming pool, half full of jelly, that Bendryn kept looking at rather nervously for signs of life.

They sipped their drinks and nibbled their crisps until Bendryn noticed two large breasted and bikini-clad women climb into the pool. He sat there agog as they began to grapple one another and writhe around in the jiggling mass. He was suddenly pleased he hadn't embarrassed himself by saying anything about 'live jelly' out loud, and yet he was sure he heard Rudolph titter.

They watched in open-mouthed amazement as the women grabbed each other by the arms or the hair or whatever they could get hold of in an effort to pull each other down into the jelly. The crowd was cheering them on, whistling and chanting while the women were working themselves into a messy frenzy in the wibbly wobbling mass.

Soon enough the bikini tops had come adrift enough for Bendryn to get a good look at his first naked breasts. He was mesmerised by the bountiful bouncing mounds of jelly covered flesh and he wanted nothing more than to touch one and lick the sweet sticky mess off it. That thought, and the way the women were still grappling with practically naked, slippery bodies long after they were both completely covered from head to toe in sloppy melting jelly, made Bendryn's toes quiver. It caused the little bells on the upturned tips of his boots to tinkle, a sure sign that he was getting excited.

He found himself cheering and whistling and tried to push his way closer just as one woman managed to lift the other up and slam her down into what was left of the jelly sending a wave of stickiness over the nearby patrons including Bendryn and Rudolph.

As the women got out of the pool and headed away, Bendryn lost his head and went to lunge at one but was stopped by an enormous hand grabbing the back of his clothes. It was the three-toothed guy from the door. He said, "Look but don't touch, Kermit, or you'll be late."

"Late for what?" Bendryn asked, puzzled.

"Late as in, the late whatever your name is." The big man laughed and walked away.

Bendryn pulled himself together and went back to the table with Rudolph who seemed to have bought more drinks despite having no money with him. Bendryn was feeling rather sticky and uncomfortable now and really wished he had thought to bring his towel with him. But they had left in a hurry. They sipped in silence as the crowd dispersed and then the lighting changed to illuminate a stage close by.

The music got louder and started to really pump. The crowd began to whistle and cheer again as a very fit young woman climbed up on the stage. Almost instantly she began gyrating suggestively and peeling off parts of her clothing and Bendryn was spellbound. He just stared in amazement as the young woman danced and undressed right there on the stage in front of all those men. When she was down to her very skimpy underwear, she grabbed hold of a pole in the middle of the stage and began doing the most amazing acrobatics, close to naked and close to Bendryn and all but blew his mind.

Bendryn lost his head again and lunged at the stage. Petunia thought *'oh no not again,'* but Bendryn was stopped by a wall with three teeth.

"I told you Gumby, look but don't touch," the bouncer said, holding Bendryn by the throat.

Bendryn was sure the big guy was going to snap him in half and throw both ends out into the street. However, Rudolph locked eyes with the bouncer and the big man put Bendryn down gently instead. "If you want to actually touch a girl, you best go upstairs. We got rules, you know? You don't touch the girls down here. But up there..." He pointed straight up and laughed. "Up there... you got the money, you can have pretty much anything your jolly green heart might desire."

Bendryn liked the sound of that.

Bendryn and Rudolph headed up a red carpeted staircase with some trepidation and a little bit of shandy induced unsteadiness. They were met at the top by a buxom, flame-haired woman. She was older than the others they had seen, Bendryn thought, but he was no great judge of these things. She looked them both up and down slowly and said, "I see you enjoyed the jelly wrestling."

Bendryn looked down at his lovely green elf threads and realised he was in a bit of a mess, but he was on a mission. He needed to find a very naughty girl before Santa called him home, so he decided to ignore the state of his clothes.

"I'd like to touch a naughty girl...please," he said, remembering his manners. "Have I come to the right place?"

The red-headed woman raised one eyebrow slightly and said, "Indeed." Then she made a gimme type gesture and said, "How much money have you got on you, Spock?"

Bendryn suddenly felt self-conscious about his ears for some reason but emptied the rest of cousin Heldryn's gift into the woman's outstretched palm and hoped there was enough magic left for the currency to go unnoticed. Rudolph stared hard at the woman as she fondled the money and looked undecided. He stared so hard his nose glowed much brighter than usual, and the woman was distracted by it for a moment before she lifted up a telephone and made a call.

"Got one for you, honey, if you're free for a little while," she said into the handset. Then she pointed up the stairs and said, "Up you go, and Patsy will sort you out."

Bendryn and Rudolph headed unsteadily up the stairs and went to head to the left, but the red-headed woman called out, "Hang on, don't go that way, never go that way. That way leads to the dark side and you wouldn't like that." Then she chuckled to herself.

Bendryn and Rudolph headed to the right instead and were met halfway down the hall by a cute and bouncy girl who introduced herself as Patsy. She had Shirley Temple curls and was very curvy.

"Madame didn't mention your friend," she said motioning towards Rudolph.

"She sent us both up after we paid," Bendryn replied quite truthfully as Rudolph stared at the woman.

"Guess you better both come in then," she said cheerily and led them into a small neat room with a bed and a chair. She turned to Bendryn and said, "So what is it you want honey?"

Bendryn suddenly felt shy and tongue-tied. He looked down at the floor and quietly said, "I'd like to touch a naughty girl."

Patsy didn't seem at all put off by that. She took him by the hand and led him to the bed where she sat him down and then sat next to him.

Rudolph just tried to look inconspicuous in the corner.

Patsy undid the buttons of her shirt matter of factly and took it off. Bendryn had his first close up view of naked breasts and he was completely awestruck. He thought that if Santa called him back now, he could die a happy elf.

Patsy took one of Bendryn's hands and placed it on the milky white flesh. "Go on," she whispered. "Touch me."

Bendryn squeezed the soft flesh and felt the nipple begin to contract and harden. He was afraid he had done something wrong and took his hand away. Patsy laughed, not unkindly, and gestured for him to put his hand back.

He lifted both his hands, placed one gently on each breast, and began to squeeze them and knead them gently, watching the nipples change and become hard nubs. He looked up at Patsy, checking she was okay for him to continue, and she nodded and smiled.

Bendryn was spellbound but growing in confidence. He started to fondle the flesh more and tweak the nipples to see just how hard they could get. All the while Patsy waited patiently, watching him play like a kid with a new puppy... or two.

She smiled softly at him and said: "You can kiss them you know."

Bendryn almost melted at the thought and his toes started to quiver, making his bells tinkle. He approached one breast very slowly with his lips, almost afraid he would startle it if he moved too quickly. When in truth it was more likely he would startle himself. Finally, his lips touched the soft, warm flesh, and his bells tinkled louder than they ever had. He kissed it tenderly all over, saving the nipple until last, then kissed it and ran his tongue over it.

His bells were practically ringing and he was getting more and more bold with every moment. He licked and kissed and sucked and fiddled and fondled and kneaded like a kid with new play dough. He rolled his face around in the warm, soft mounds, and at one point he even sat them on his head.

Finally, Patsy said, "Times up I'm afraid, I have to get ready for a party."

Bendryn's heart sank at the thought of leaving those beautiful breasts, but he and Rudolph reluctantly left the room. Safe in the knowledge that they had finally met a proper naughty girl before they got recalled.

They went to head back down the stairs and go home but suddenly Rudolph's head went up, and his nostrils flared as if he was picking up a scent, and he made a move to dash back the other way.

"No, no Rudolph. No, that way leads to the dark side!" Bendryn warned and tried to hold the deer back. Then he smelled it too and realised they were in deep trouble. Bendryn realised that Rudolph had caught the scent of peanut butter and his heart sank.

Peanut butter was known to be an almost irresistible aphrodisiac for magic reindeer. So much so that children in the North Pole had been banned from having it on their school lunches after a particularly ugly incident when Bendryn's great, great Aunt had sent her children off to school with poorly wrapped, crunchy peanut butter sandwiches in the middle of the rutting season.

Some of the students and teachers that were there that day were still in therapy, and several of the deer have been in and out of rehab ever since.

Rudolph would normally abstain, being a generally sensible deer, but with a couple of shandies and half a packet of crisps on board, Bendryn knew it was a lost cause. The force was too strong but he bravely tried to hold his friend back for as long as he could until Rudolph literally dragged Bendryn kicking and screaming to the dark side. Or at least to the door of the dark side. Or at least to a door with a sign on it that said, *'The Dark Side- Dungeon and Private Rooms Available for Hire.'*

Rudolph paused only briefly before barrelling through the door in search of smooth nutty goodness.

What they saw was enough to even stop an overexcited magic reindeer in his tracks. They were in a large room that looked like an arena and there was activity everywhere. It took Bendryn a few moments to focus and work out what he was seeing then he realised it was some sort of chariot race with people yelling and placing bets as the competitors were getting set up on the starting line.

The chariots were tremendous and varied in size from small single person ones to large ones with three or more people in them. Each of the chariots had a driver, and each driver was elaborately dressed and held some form of whip, but the thing that stopped Rudolph and froze both he and Bendryn were the 'horses' pulling the chariots. They were people and almost all of them naked but for bits, bridles, and harnesses. One chariot had six beautiful young women harnessed to it with their leather all polished and shiny, their hair plaited like sled horse's tails on fair day, and each of them wore a coloured feather on a headdress.

Bendryn was dumbstruck as he looked them up and down and noticed how meticulously they had been prepared for the race. Right down to the special shoes that made them stand up on shiny gold hooves that matched the trimmings on the chariot. They kept lifting their feet and jostling about like real ponies. Bendryn thought they were lovely.

The next chariot had a mixture of young men and women. Again, dressed and harnessed with a great deal of care and attention to detail. Their hooves were black and only the lead ponies had headdresses with black feathers. The rest had intricate plaits in their hair that looked like manes with tiny bells worked into them, so they tinkled when they tossed their heads about. Which they seemed to do a lot.

The last chariot that Bendryn could see clearly was being pulled by one enormous man, harnessed in brown leather, wearing not much other than thick brown boots with a slightly different style of hoof. He was wearing horns and pawing at the ground impatiently, and Bendryn realised he was a bullock or an ox.

The energy in the room was reaching fever pitch, and Rudolph and Bendryn were still virtually paralysed as a bell went off to start the race. Bendryn could see the muscles straining as the ponies and the ox pulled the chariots as fast as they could around the arena, spurred on by the whips and the cries of the drivers.

As they went past, Bendryn could smell the sweat and see the strain and the urge to win. The crowd was screaming, and the drivers were ruthless with their whips. A loud cry went up as they crossed the finish line almost in a pack. Bendryn had no idea who won, but his heart was pounding at the excitement anyway.

There was so much activity it was hard to see what was happening. People and ponies were everywhere. Some being unharnessed, some being rubbed down, some just prancing on the spot in their harnesses.

One driver had bent one of her pretty pony girls over and was rubbing her between her legs. Bendryn wasn't sure what he was seeing, but it started to dawn on him when another driver walked towards his pony with his pants undone and made her bend over. Just as the ox was driven to his knees by a leather-clad woman with a riding crop, two things happened at once.

Firstly, Rudolph got the renewed scent of peanut butter as somebody was smearing it on small slices of apple and feeding it to the ponies. That shook the deer out of his reverie. His head went up, his nose began to glow brightly, and he stared hard at the person with the jar. Bendryn could tell Rudolph was about to bolt.

The second thing that happened was that Bendryn's toes began to quiver and his ringing bells could even be heard over all the raucous goings-on.

So just as Rudolph bolted for the pony pack where somebody was now smearing peanut butter over the naked buttocks of a pretty pony, an enormous woman with a whip picked Bendryn up by the scruff of his green elf shirt, and said: "Private party, Paddy, and you ain't invited." She threw him out the door, slamming it behind him.

Bendryn landed hard up against the banister and was quite dazed. When he gathered his thoughts, he decided Rudolph could take care of himself but Bendryn couldn't get home without him. So, he decided to wait downstairs in the bar and hope Rudolph got kicked out not far behind him. He got up and headed the way he thought they had come, but he was feeling a little disoriented and ended up in a dead-end hallway with nowhere else to go but through a closed door. 'Curiouser and curiouser' he thought to himself 'I was sure that was the way out'.

When he went to turn back, he wasn't sure which way he had come. He felt dazed and a little sick, and he heard an odd noise, sort of a whooshing, slapping sound that seemed to be calling to him from behind the door. At the same time, he thought he heard footsteps behind him and angry voices. He was suddenly scared he was about to be in trouble for being in the wrong place.

He looked around for somewhere to go, somewhere to hide, but whichever way he moved the angry voices seemed to be coming from that direction. It was like he was being herded into the dead end. Finally, he found himself pressed up against the closed door and the sound coming from it was now a clear, rhythmic whoosh, slap. Followed by a muffled whimper and the sound was growing louder...and calling Bendryn through the door.

He was sure he shouldn't go in there. But the angry voices now seemed to be coming from all directions and getting closer, and the sound from the other side of the door was so appealing he couldn't help it.

He opened the door slowly and carefully to step inside. It took a moment for his eyes to adjust to the light and then all he could do was stare. He couldn't move; he was frozen to the spot, staring. The first thing he noticed was an enormous rectangular wooden frame made from exquisite timber. The second thing he saw was what enthralled him. A woman; a naked woman. A beautiful tall, slender woman, bound at the wrists, ankles, and waist, suspended within the frame. Her blond hair was hanging loosely around her face. She looked like a delicate flower, suspended. Bound and suspended to become an ethereal work of living art.

Bendryn stood still and studied her. Her wrists were bound by canvas straps that were nailed to the top corners of the frame. Her ankles were in metal shackles that were locked and chained to the bottom corners.

Her waist was held firmly by a wide ornate belt or brace with metal rings on each side to which steel rods protruding from the frame were attached.

She could have been an exotic butterfly caught in a devious and diabolical web. Tears were streaming down her cheeks, and her alabaster limbs were stretching, straining, like a ballerina on pointe or like an angel reaching out to heaven. A beautiful fallen angel. A weeping angel.

'Don't blink', Bendryn thought to himself. 'She must be an apparition, and if I blink, she will vanish.' As soon as he thought that, of course, he had to blink. But the framed girl was still there when he opened his eyes and the sound continued. Whoosh, slap, followed by an exquisite whimper from the mouth of the suspended siren.

Bendryn was mesmerised and stood very still, trying to work out what was going on. He was terrified of being caught where he was not meant to be, but he needed to work out what was making the rest of the noise. He slowly worked his way around the room trying to get to the other side of the frame. Keeping himself close to the wall and trying to be as stealthy as a slightly tipsy elf with bells on his shoes can be.

He followed the sound around the wall. It was gradually getting louder and louder and each whimper was beginning to make the hairs on the back of his neck stand up, in a good way.

Finally, he could see the other side of the frame and saw another tall, willowy woman standing there. She was the same build as the blonde woman, but her hair was darker, more a golden brown with a reddish tinge when she moved in the light, and she wasn't naked.

But she might as well have been. Her tiny red sleeveless dress was so short it barely covered her bottom and fitted her so snuggly that Bendryn could see every curve and every muscle as it moved under the shiny red latex. She took a step forward and he froze, fearful that he had been spotted, but she didn't look at him. Her feet were encased in the brightest red suede boots Bendryn had ever seen. Short boots that came just to the ankle and had the thinnest of stiletto heels. Bendryn couldn't imagine how anybody could walk in anything so high. But she seemed to be managing it beautifully.

The shoes gave way to white stockings that Bendryn's eyes followed all the way up to the band of white faux fur trim at the top which seemed to be holding very firmly to her legs. As his eyes continued to trace their way up over her strong slender thighs, he noticed the skirt was trimmed in the same white fur, and so was the Santa style hat that she was wearing, the colour of which matched her bright red lipstick perfectly.

Bendryn panicked as the woman stepped forward again and raised her arm with something in her hand before she brought it down sharply with a whooshing sound. It landed across the naked back of the suspended girl with a slap, causing her to emit a delicious whimper.

Bendryn knew that was the sound he had been hearing, but it took a few moments for him to process what he was seeing.

She stood there, legs slightly apart, and raised her arm again. This time Bendryn could see that she was holding a handle with a short length of chain attached and at the other end of the chain was a bunch of brightly coloured, pointed leather straps, fastened together in a way that made it look like a giant rainbow coloured squid but with a lot more legs.

There were maybe a couple of dozen straps and as he watched, she brought them down across the back of the framed girl. He heard the whoosh, slap, whimper and he realised he was watching one beautiful woman administer a flogging to the other.

The feelings that gave him were like nothing he had ever experienced before, and he wasn't sure he could explain them, not even to himself. The lash came down again and again, each time leaving long red pointed marks on the body of the bound woman. On her back and her thighs and the cheeks of her bottom. Each lash leaving dozens of red marks on the white flesh. Like a painter was painting a canvas. One woman, the framed work of art and the other, the artist.

The sounds increased in intensity with the increasing vigour of the action and soon Bendryn found his toes began to quiver and his bells began to ring, and he knew he was about to be discovered. He was torn between trying to explain himself and running, and he had just decided to put his head down and run when he heard the most enchanting voice he had ever encountered.

"Don't run."

Bendryn froze on the spot realising that they must have known he was there all along. He took a deep breath and raised his head. When he looked over, the golden-haired woman in the red latex dress was standing with her head cocked to one side and a cheeky looking grin on her face.

"Please don't go," she said. "We'd like you to stay and watch."

Bendryn was only partly sure he was not dreaming, and not at all sure he was not about to be flogged himself, but he tried to relax.

"She likes it when I let people watch," the woman said in a reassuring tone. "Truly, we'd like you to stay."

She smiled beautifully and crooked her finger at the elf to beckon him closer. Something in her smile and her voice made him feel all warm and gooey inside, and he decided to trust her.

He took a couple of steps forward and she beckoned some more.

"Has she been very bad?" he asked, as he stepped closer.

"Bad?" she said. "No, not at all. In fact, she has been very, very good"

"Then, why?" was all he could manage

"This?" she asked holding up the flogger. "This is our Christmas present." She chuckled just a little. "And we are having our own private Christmas party. Can't you tell?" She stood in a model like pose and moved her hand in the air up and down her body like a game show hostess showing off a prize.

Bendryn was still confused and worried about the crying girl. "But she is crying," he said.

"Yes, but she can stop me anytime she wants, truly she can. She has a safe word that will stop me straight away," the woman replied.

Bendryn was bewildered and fascinated and he didn't know what else.

"I was about to turn her over," the woman said, "Would you like to help me?"

Bendryn was nervous, aroused, and confused, but he nodded and stepped closer, then closer again as the golden-haired woman said, "What's your name honey?"

"Bendryn Elford," the elf replied nervously.

"Pleased to meet you Bendryn Elford," she said as she tucked the flogger under her arm and reached out to shake Bendryn's hand. "I'm Miesha and this is Strawberry." She pointed to the woman in the frame. "If you could turn that handle there for me that would be a big help."

Bendryn looked at the crank handle Miesha had pointed to at the side of the frame. He pulled out a locking pin and turned the handle slowly. As he did so the frame tilted and began to turn. He briefly thought about the wonderful craftsmanship as the frame reached a horizontal position with the naked Strawberry now facing the ceiling.

He fastened the locking pin and stood to admire the beautiful blond woman now stretched out before him.

"You can touch her if you'd like," Miesha said

Bendryn looked up at her to check he understood her correctly and she nodded with a smile.

The elf was not sure if he dared to touch something so beautiful, but he remembered that he could be recalled at any moment and he did not want to go home with any regrets, so he reached his hand out slowly and carefully and tentatively touched Strawberry's arm, ever so lightly. He heard her moan a little and he withdrew his hand instantly.

"It's okay," Miesha said. "She likes it when I let people touch her and she can stop us if she wants to. Relax. Touch her."

Miesha's voice was so soothing and Strawberry looked so beautiful spread out before him that he summoned up the courage to reach out and touch her arm again. This time he traced his fingertips down to her shoulder and then along her torso. He was not game enough to touch her breasts, but Miesha stepped over and took one of Strawberry's nipples between her thumb and fingers and twisted it hard.

Bendryn felt a bolt of something go through his entire body when he saw that and heard the sound Strawberry made. He was afraid at first, but Miesha said, "Relax, Bendryn. May I call you Bendryn?"

The elf nodded.

"Relax. She likes it, trust me" Miesha was practically purring as she twisted Strawberry's nipple again even harder and the bound blonde woman moaned. Bendryn feared he might drool.

Miesha ran a red painted fingernail along Strawberry's body until her hand bumped into Bendryn's, then she walked around him until she was standing at the foot of the frame. Bendryn watched her; the way she walked in those boots was sending tingles through him. She looked pensive for a moment then reached and took his hand.

"Come on honey, let's have a little fun," she said as she ducked under the frame and popped up between Strawberry's outstretched legs.

Bendryn followed with his heart beating so hard he was afraid Santa would hear it and realise he was up to no good. He found himself standing within the frame, between Strawberry's legs and pressed quite close to Miesha, seeing parts of Strawberry's body he had never even imagined when he stole the naughty list. His grandmother's words echoed in his head: "Be careful what you wish for." His heart beating way too loudly in his ears.

"Go on, Bendryn, touch her."

"I...I...I don't know how," the elf stammered

"Here," Miesha said softly, taking his hand. "I'll show you."

Bendryn let her lift his hand to the soft skin of Strawberry's taut belly.

"Soft isn't she?" Miesha said quietly "It's okay if you want to touch her lower."

Bendryn was trembling and could barely breathe, let alone move. Miesha took his hand again and said, "Shh, relax, it is all okay. Here, move down and feel her, she will like that."

Miesha moved Bendryn's hand down lower across the soft, smooth flesh to a small triangle of neatly trimmed hair covering her soft mound. His bells were ringing practically off his boots and Miesha smiled at him lasciviously as she moved his hand lower still. Bendryn heard Strawberry moan softly, but this time he didn't pull away. He let Miesha guide his nervous but eager fingers down to the soft lips between Strawberry's legs.

Bendryn was trembling all over, not just his toes, as Miesha moved his hand slowly and gently, encouraging his fingers to trail along the edge of Strawberry's secret folds, causing her to emit soft sounds that made Bendryn's heart flutter.

Miesha changed the position of her hand over Bendryn's, extending one of his fingers out and pressing hers along side it to guide him.

His breathing was so hard and heavy he thought he might faint.

"Relax, honey," Miesha crooned softly in his ear. "We'll all like this, I promise."

She rested her other hand on Strawberry's neatly trimmed patch and used her fingers to part the soft, lips. She moved hers and Bendryn's fingers just between the folds until he could feel how warm and wet Strawberry was. He was so amazed at the smooth slipperiness of her that he made a little sound, one that made Miesha chuckle softly.

She moved their hands until Bendryn's fingers were all slippery and wet, then she parted Strawberry's lips a little more and said, "Here, Bendryn, touch her here," as she guided his fingers so that the tip slid gently over a small hard nub.

The sound Strawberry made was like a symphony of birdsong wafting through his soul and he wanted to hear more. Miesha obliged, moving their fingers over and around what seemed to Bendryn to be a magic button, making Strawberry all but sing.

The area of slippery wetness seemed to be expanding and soon both Miesha and Bendryn's hands were slick with it while Strawberry seemed to be in an ecstatic passion. Miesha changed position of her hand again slightly and moved Bendryn's finger to rest along two of hers. "Hold it straight honey," she whispered as she moved it a little lower and deeper between Strawberry's soft, slippery lips and pushed it slowly, with her own fingers, deep inside the beautiful bound woman.

The sound all three of them made was accompanied by the ringing of Bendryn's bells which only got louder and more rhythmic as Miesha slid their fingers deep into Strawberry, again and again until Bendryn feared he might die of excitement. He could feel the tight warmth of Strawberry surrounding his finger and squeezing him harder against Miesha's. It was a feeling he had never even imagined before and he did briefly wonder if it was a feeling anybody had ever felt before.

"I think that will do her for now," Miesha said as she slid their fingers slowly out of Strawberry. "Don't want to make her orgasm now, do we?"

Bendryn was pleased that sounded like a rhetorical question because he had not the foggiest idea how to respond.

"But I have an idea how to make this more Christmassy before we finish her flogging if you would like to help me," Miesha said with a lascivious lilt.

The elf could only nod. He was sure he had never felt quite so overwhelmed before.

"Help me off with my boots, Bendryn," Miesha said in a deliciously bossy tone.

Bendryn knelt in the confined space and removed the gorgeous red suede boots, one at a time. Then looked up at Miesha for his next instruction. She was towering over him, tall and slender but strong, like an Amazonian archer. She put one foot on his thigh and said, "Take off my stocking now."

Bendryn loved the confident tone of her voice. He reached both hands up either side of her muscled thigh to get hold of the fur band at the top of her stocking and carefully slid it down her smooth leg. She pulled her foot out of the last of it and put her hand out. Bendryn handed her the still warm stocking. Then she changed legs and the process was repeated.

She slid her feet back into the boots and put out her hand to help Bendryn up. The look on her face was something he couldn't fathom, like a playful naughtiness but with a slightly dark edge. She said, "So, given that this is a Christmas party, I propose some stocking stuffing."

She crooked her finger for Bendryn to come closer and then slowly dragged the whole length of the stocking through her hand as if straightening it out. She took Bendryn's hand in hers, held his fingers out straight and put the toe of the stocking between the tips.

"Here honey, I'll start you off," she said, spreading Strawberry's wet lips apart and pressing Bendryn's fingers just inside. "Now you do it, honey, I want you to stuff it into her" Bendryn's eyes grew wide when he understood what she wanted, and she chuckled. "Yes, Bendryn. I want you to stuff that stocking deep inside our hot girl."

Strawberry and Bendryn moaned in unison as he began to push the fine white fabric deep into her, bit by bit. Pressing it in as deep as he could with each inward movement and trying not to let it come back out as he withdrew. Little by little it vanished inside of her and little by little Bendryn could feel the level of arousal in the room growing.

Eventually, the fur band was the only part of the stocking still visible, and Bendryn thought he was finished.

"Don't stop there" Miesha said in a breathless voice "Stuff it all in, all the way. She can take it, stuff it in hard."

Bendryn's bells were ringing louder than he had ever heard before but he could only just make them out over the sound of Strawberry's moans and his own beating heart. He pushed and shoved the last of the stocking, not really believing it would fit, but with some effort, it all eventually vanished into Strawberry's hot wet depths.

Bendryn felt a surge of triumph, excitement and arousal that left him quite dizzy, as Miesha took his hand, and led him back out of the frame and up to Strawberry's head. Miesha licked the last of the tear stains off Strawberry's cheeks then kissed her mouth. Bendryn wasn't sure where to look but he did notice the contrast in their lipsticks. Strawberry's was more of a coral pink colour rather than red like Miesha's, and when he looked to check he noticed Strawberry's nails matched her lips just the way that Miesha's did

Miesha lifted her head back up and ran the second stocking through her hand as she had done with the first. "My turn now, I think," she said as she toyed with the toe of the stocking with her fingers. She gripped Strawberry's jaw and forced her mouth open. "Tongue back, lovely," she ordered. "Don't want you to choke." Then she began to feed the stocking bit by bit into the open mouth, pressing it in the same way Bendryn had done but between different lips.

Bendryn watched in fascination as the long slender fingers of one woman manipulated the white fabric between the coral pink lips of the other. He wasn't sure it would all fit when it came to the fur band, but it did. Just. Miesha then kissed Strawberry gently on the forehead and said: "Okay, Bendryn honey, time to spin her the rest of the way around."

Bendryn went to the crank, took out the locking pin and began to turn. The frame and Strawberry began to move until she was virtually upside down.

"That's good," Miesha said. "Just a bit more and lock her there."

Bendryn did as he was told and then beat a hasty retreat as he noticed Miesha had her flogger in her hand again and was looking very stern. He stood where he would be out of the way but where he could see clearly. Something was bothering him, so he got up the courage to speak.

"How will she tell you if she wants you to stop?"

"Don't worry Bendryn honey, she has hand signals she can use. She is perfectly safe," Miesha reassured him. "Besides, I know her limits and today is a party, not punishment so she will be fine."

Bendryn relaxed, a little...and then it began. Gently at first, almost soundless lashes across her torso and the front of her thighs, barely leaving any sort of mark at all. But as Miesha warmed up, the whooshing sound returned and soon the slapping sound and then the whimpering as each lash left bright red lines across every part of Strawberry; her thighs, her belly, her breasts…everywhere but her face.

Bendryn began to really admire the control that Miesha had over her art. He realised that every blow landed exactly where she wanted it. Exactly where it was needed to add to the artwork, to make the colour even and balanced and he thought that they must do this a lot for her to be so skilled. He was suddenly brought back to himself when the tone of the whimpering changed into more of a muffled yelping sound as Miesha changed her angle and was lashing Strawberry between her legs, on her inner thighs, on her soft wet lips, and her hair covered mound.

Bendryn found himself surrounded by a sea of sounds, the whooshing slapping sound of the lash, the sounds of Strawberry's whimpering and muffled yelping, and the sound of his own bells playing a loud rhythmic tune he had never heard before in concert with the rest. He felt like Miesha was not just 'painting' Strawberry. She was playing her like she was a beautiful instrument, an ornate harp or a rare baroque harpsichord, and his bells were the accompaniment.

Miesha continued until there was barely a part of Strawberry left unmarked. When she finally stopped, Bendryn could practically feel the warm glow emanating from the newly reddened skin and it gave him a thrilling tingle all over his own.

"Wind her onto her back for me, Bendryn, honey," Miesha said. "I think she deserves a little treat."

Bendryn turned Strawberry back to the horizontal position, on her back, and locked the crank. Miesha walked along the length of the frame, admiring her handy work. Then she ducked under the edge again and beckoned to Bendryn.

"Come and watch me nice and close honey," she said with a voice practically dripping with seduction.

Bendryn ducked under and was once again positioned between the helpless Strawberry's legs. Miesha winked at him then she leant over and kissed Strawberry just below her navel, then kissed her way down Strawberry's belly and across her mound. When Bendryn finally realised what he was about to witness, he had to put his hand on the frame to steady himself.

Miesha kissed the soft lips, put her hands up to part them, and ran her tongue along where Bendryn had not long before had his fingers. He could see the white fur of the stocking top peeking out at him and a bolt of pleasure shimmered through him. All three of them moaned as Miesha moved her focus to the small nub that had given Strawberry so much pleasure before.

Bendryn watched spellbound as Miesha's tongue flicked and glided over the magic button with ever-increasing intensity until Strawberry was straining against her bonds and making the most deliciously urgent sounds through the stocking still stuffed into her mouth. Each time it seemed Strawberry was reaching some sort of pinnacle, Miesha paused her actions and grinned a close-to-evil-grin and then started again, slower and with less intensity then worked her way back up to near fever pitch.

Bendryn lost track of how many times Miesha build it up and then started again. He had eventually worked out what was going on and he was almost exhausted from anticipation by the time it seemed that Miesha looked like she was going to let Strawberry go all the way to her climax.

Strawberry was struggling and straining against her confines and making sounds that Bendryn now realised were the muffled sounds of pleading. He knew Strawberry was begging for release and that excited him immensely.

Finally, Miesha's activity became close to frantic and she put her hands on Strawberry's thighs and squeezed so hard it almost made Bendryn's eyes water. Suddenly he saw just about every muscle in Strawberry's body tighten as she totally froze under Miesha's tongue. Silent, as if holding her breath, waiting. Then she screamed with such glorious victory and release that not even the stocking in her mouth could muffle the cry.

Her whole body shuddered, and it felt like Bendryn could feel it in his own bones. Then a similar shudder ran through Miesha and he felt that too. He felt the connection between the women. The artist and the art, as if they were two sides of the same coin. As if they were one.

When Bendryn came back to himself, he saw Miesha resting her head on Strawberry's belly; they were both panting but not as heavily as they were before

"Here," Miesha said taking the elf's hand. "Take it out for her honey," she motioned her head towards where Bendryn had put the stocking. He swallowed hard, took a deep breath, and took hold of the white fur just poking out from between the soft wet lips. He drew out the white, now wet material slowly and carefully, eliciting a sigh of relief from the still bound woman.

He was so absorbed in what he was doing he hadn't noticed Miesha move to Strawberry's head. When he looked up, she was slowly pulling the stocking from her mouth. Then she kissed her with a passion that made him blush and look down at his feet.

"Don't be shy with us, Bendryn," Miesha said. "We like you. Come, help me get her out of this frame."

The two of them set to work. It was trickier than he expected, she was very well nailed and secured in place, but he was a painting and construction elf, after all so he was good with tools.

Once they had Strawberry out of the frame, they had to help her stand. She was quite wobbly on her feet. They guided her to a lounge by the wall and sat her down. Miesha took a blanket out of a colourful carpet bag on the floor, put it around Strawberry's shoulders, then sat beside her. She put her arm around Strawberry and the pretty blonde rested her head on the offered shoulder and snuggled in.

"Could you pour us some tea please, Bendryn?" Miesha motioned towards the bag. "There should be a thermos in there."

Bendryn went searching in the seemingly bottomless bag and eventually found a flask of tea.

"There should be some sugar in there, too. She usually prefers honey, but spill one drop of the stuff and you keep finding it on everything you put in that bag for months." Miesha chuckled.

Bendryn found a small container of sugar cubes and, under instruction, some cheese and crackers and a packet of chocolate biscuits. He poured tea into two cups he found in the bag and poured one for himself into the lid of the flask.

Miesha pulled a face as she sipped hers.

"Is it okay?" Bendryn asked nervously

"Yes, honey." She smiled kindly. "It's fine, it is just that I usually prefer earl grey hot. But it has been in the thermos for hours, so it can't be helped."

Strawberry sipped her tea, then looked up at Bendryn with glassy eyes and said, "Thank you, Bendryn."

Her voice was much like Miesha's but softer and he realised it was the first time he had heard her speak. She smiled at him. She looked tired but happy.

They drank their tea and Miesha fed Strawberry some snacks then held her as Bendryn, under instruction, rubbed her ankles and wrists until she fell asleep. They sat there in convivial silence for a while until Strawberry stirred. "Don't we have to get ready for the party?" she asked a little anxiously.

"As soon as you're up to it beautiful, no rush. Okay?" Miesha said and kissed her on the forehead.

When Strawberry was ready, Miesha helped her into a pretty, floral dress and then they packed everything into the bag and went to leave.

Bendryn just stood there, a little lost, not sure where he should go or what he should do. He thought he should go and look for Rudolph; he was bound to be waiting somewhere.

As the girls were just about at the door, they turned around and almost in unison said, "Are you coming, Bendryn?"

He suddenly perked up and scrambled to catch up with them. Miesha took his hand and said, "We have to work so we can't be mingling much at the party." Both girls giggled at what seemed like a private joke. "But you can wait with us while we get ready and then come along as our guest if you like."

"I'd like that," Bendryn replied, becoming increasingly nervous that Santa may call him back any moment and the girls would think he had just vanished on them. "I... I may vanish," he stammered, trying to keep up with the long-legged beauties. "And I won't mean to...I just. Well, I just might"

The girls stopped walking and Strawberry looked at him solemnly. "What's the matter Bendryn? I thought you liked us. We like you."

"Yes," he said. "I like you a lot, but-but-but I may vanish. It won't be my fault, but it might just happen. Here take this in case, please"

Bendryn reached into his inner pocket and handed them a business card that read:

'Bendryn Elford- Third Assistant Sub-Apprentice to the Second Vice-Head of Painting and Construction. Mail, c/o Santa. North Pole'

Miesha read the card, smiled, and handed it to Strawberry who said, "I have no idea what any of that means but some of those words are my favourites." Both the girls laughed beautifully, and Strawberry put the card in the pocket of her dress.

"Now come along," they said, and each took one of Bendryn's hands while they headed off to the party.

Bendryn didn't know where they were taking him, nor did he care. He was happy to have two beautiful, practically perfect, naughty girls holding his hands and didn't care where they went, Now, he at least felt that if he vanished, they could contact him if they wanted to. He had the cards made up as soon as Santa told him of his impending promotion, although now he wasn't sure he would need them. He was going to be in so much trouble when he got home. But he decided not to think about that.

They turned corners, went down some stairs and up others, and at times Bendryn felt like the staircases were moving or like he was in one of those pictures where the hand was drawing itself. Finally, they went through a set of large swinging doors and were in what looked like a busy industrial kitchen. A large, ruddy-faced man was ordering people about in a Jamaican accent.

"Where have you two been?" he almost yelled at the girls, and then without waiting for an answer, he said, "Go and get ready. We are waiting for you."

The girls still had hold of Bendryn's hands as they headed to get ready. Miesha leant over and whispered, "Don't worry, that's just Sebastian. He's always a bit crabby. But he's mostly harmless."

They led him into a large changing room with lockers and hooks on the wall to hang clothes opposite a line of showers. The girls proceeded to undress. Bendryn didn't know where to look so he started to stare at his feet.

"Don't look down, please, Bendryn," Miesha said. "We want you to watch…please."

The elf looked up shyly but was determined to make his new friends happy.

He watched carefully as Miesha helped Strawberry out of her dress. Then Strawberry began peeling Miesha's clothes off, slowly and carefully like she was unwrapping a gift. Miesha's body was much like Strawberry's, long and lean and beautiful, and by the time they were both naked Bendryn was totally smitten with them.

Strawberry whispered something he didn't hear, then both girls smiled at him and giggled. They approached and stood either side of him and kissed him on opposite cheeks. Miesha said, "Strawberry thinks we have time for a little fun. Do you trust us? We won't hurt you."

Bendryn had no clue what they had in mind, but he really didn't care. He nodded eagerly.

"Close your eyes honey," Strawberry purred. "We won't hurt you, I promise."

He closed his eyes and felt soft lips on his cheeks again, then on his ears which tickled a little, then on his nose, and then he felt soft sweet kisses on his lips, and his knees almost melted. He wasn't sure how to respond, but he just went with the feeling and did what felt good. Soon he had two warm mouths exploring his. They tasted of chocolate and tea and he didn't know who was who, but it didn't matter. The soft wet lips, the probing caressing tongues, it all felt so good he began to tremble and his bells began to ring.

"Keep your eyes closed honey. We are going to see just how much we can make those bells ring." He thought it was Miesha that spoke, but he wasn't sure.

The girls lifted his arms up above his head and tied his wrists to the hooks above him. He felt quite nervous, but he heard a soft whisper in his ear. "Relax, Bendryn, honey. We are not going to hurt you."

So, he relaxed as much as the situation would permit.

The girls began to kiss him again. He felt fully immersed in the warmth of their sweet mouths, lips, and tongues. He kissed them back eagerly as they began to rub their hands over his chest and stomach. Then down his thighs. The kisses grew hotter, hungrier, and Bendryn felt like he may be consumed by them. He felt the girls move their hands to the inside of his thighs and then...then they touched him, touched him there!

Bendryn gasped. Both girls giggled. "Do you want us to stop, Bendryn?" one of them whispered into his ear.

"No, no, not at all, please don't stop," Bendryn said, and the girls laughed beautifully.

"Good, because we quite like men in tights." They giggled as they ran their hands over his private parts, making him grow very hard. "And you feel so big and hard in there Bendryn, I think we need to take a look."

He felt one or both of the girls pull down the front of his tights to expose his now rigid elfhood. They ooed and aaahed at it. "You are so big," they said. "And so hard," they remarked as they stroked and fondled him into a near frenzy. "And you look so delicious." They giggled and he could feel them change their positions.

Next thing he knew, Bendryn could feel their soft warm mouths and tongues eagerly exploring his erection and all manner of private areas that he had never had anybody touch, let alone two beautiful naked women. Just when he thought it couldn't get any better one of them took the head of his elfhood deep into her warm wet mouth, and the other was licking and sucking his shaft lower down.

The sound of his bells was almost deafening as the girls worked in tandem to bring him the most amazing pleasure he had ever experienced, finally working him into a lather of weeping, moaning ecstasy. His sweat soaked body trembled all over as they licked and sucked him to a shuddering climax that he would never forget.

"You can open your eyes now, Bendryn" a soft voice spoke. He was sure it was Strawberry. He opened his eyes to see the two angels on their knees in front of him. He smiled. He felt weak and limp and was practically hanging from the hooks his wrists were tied to. The girls got up and quickly undid him, then sat him on a bench close by, one on each side kissing him and rubbing his wrists.

Once they seemed sure he was okay, they went into a shower and set about washing each other very thoroughly. Bendryn just sat and watched them with a stupid happy grin on his face. Then he watched them dry and braid each other's hair and put on their makeup. He expected them to get dressed but instead, they stood him up, tidied him up a bit, and Miesha said, "We won't be able to speak to you at the party until all the food has been finished off. So, go and have a good time. If you are still around when we are free to party, we will find you! We promise."

"C'mon," Strawberry said. "Best get a move on or we'll have Sebastian in a lather."

They each took one of his hands and led Bendryn back out into the kitchen where people were yelling and bustling around like crazy. Bendryn couldn't make sense of it.

Sebastian came over and looked like he was going to try to shoo Bendryn out, but the girls piped up, "He is with us."

"Ha," Sebastian said, gesticulating. "It is about time somebody took you two in hand. Now here, lie down. One here and one here." He pointed to two long trolleys on wheels. "You sit there out of the way," he said to Bendryn pointing to a stool against the wall.

The girls climbed up on to the trolleys and were suddenly the centre of a flurry of activity. A black fabric bag was placed over each of their heads and the drawstring tied around their necks so that the only way he could tell who was who was by their nail polish. Miesha was dusted all over with icing sugar and then both girls were secured in place with flat u-shaped metal cuffs that were placed over their wrists and ankles and bolted to the trolleys. Then they had a larger one placed over their necks and bolted in place.

Some part of Bendryn wondered if he should be feeling shocked or surprised, but he was just feeling mellow and happy.

He watched carefully as about three or four people began building a wall around Miesha with small pieces of gingerbread, held together by icing that was being piped in between them like mortar around bricks.

He looked across at Strawberry and saw that there were small tubes running up from beneath the trolley and positioned over her breasts and her belly and thighs. He had no idea what that could be until they turned on a pump under the trolley and he saw warm melted chocolate starting to flow out of the tubes and run over her body.

Sebastian clapped his hands loudly and said, "Okay, finish her off now. Chop, chop"

Bendryn felt a moment of panic until he saw what he meant. People came from seemingly nowhere and began arranging morsels of food around Strawberry's body, presumably things to be dipped in the chocolate. Bendryn spotted berries, melon balls, marshmallows, biscuits, and liquorice. The last of these made him think of Rudolph and made him wonder where he was. Rudolph was a big fan of liquorice.

Once she was totally surrounded by all manner of nibblies, a young man placed a Christmas angel mask, complete with halo, over her already covered face. Then walked past Bendryn with a second mask. Bendryn followed him with his eyes and saw he was heading for Miesha, who was now the foundations of an impressive gingerbread house, complete with gardens.

Miesha's angel mask was put into position. Sebastian checked if her icing was dry enough then she was given a light dusting of icing sugar and both the trolleys were pushed out through some big swinging doors with Bendryn close behind them.

When his eyes adjusted to the lower light levels, he realised this must be 'the party'. There were people everywhere in all sorts of fancy dress and some not dressed in much at all. There were naked people strapped to poles at regular intervals and each had multiple candles fixed around their bodies by means of metal vines and leaves that held their arms and legs in various positions to make each one a human candelabra.

There were also multiple trolleys of food, all served on the bodies of masked people, and other naked people bound in all sorts of ways and shapes like human statuary. As Bendryn was looking around, he saw more and more people coming in and heading to what he figured was the bar to get drinks. He wandered over there to see if there was any lemonade but he was side-tracked when he saw Rudolph coming in the door, flanked on one side by one of the gold-hoofed pony girls and on the other side by one of the pony boys with the bells in his hair.

Bendryn ran to meet him. The deer was a bit glassy-eyed but was obviously pleased to see Bendryn. "Boy, am I pleased to see you," Bendryn said. Rudolph nudged him and nuzzled his hand and Bendryn added, "I think we should stay for the party. It would be rude not to" He hadn't realised he was going to say that until he did. Rudolph nodded his agreement and they headed for the bar.

It seemed to be somewhat organised chaos and Bendryn just took the first drink that was handed to him which he thought, in hindsight, might have been a mistake. Whatever it was, it warmed him to his toes but made him hiccup. Rudolph had the same and one of his pretty pony friends held it for him, so he could reach the straw. They moved off into a corner and more of the ponies and charioteers came in.

Bendryn could see the trolleys with his girls on them being moved around in the crowd. As they were wheeled past the corner he was in, he could see about half of the gingerbread was gone, exposing Miesha's naked body to anyone who wished to see it. That gave him an intense sort of thrill.

Then Strawberry was wheeled past. He watched for a few moments as the warm chocolate spilled over her, covering her breasts, pooling in her navel and between her thighs as people dipped morsels of food into it, and sometimes just their fingers. Watching strangers touching her like that sent another thrill through him.

He wanted to introduce Rudolph to his girls, but it didn't seem to be the right moment. Then a sudden realisation came over him. They were not really 'his' girls at all and as soon as Santa caught up with him, he was never likely to see them again, let alone get the chance to introduce them to anybody.

With those thoughts in his mind, he slumped into a pile of cushions and beanbags in the corner and watched Miesha and Strawberry being wheeled away into the crowd. Bendryn felt very glum until Rudolph nudged him and one of the pretty ponies sat down beside him and handed him another drink.

He was still feeling very sullen but the drink was very warming and the pony was very cute and after a little while he began to feel much more relaxed. So much so that when the pony girl moved in close to him and started stroking his neck, he decided that the girls wanted him to have a good time so he should do just that.

He quickly finished his drink then turned to the girl now stroking his ears and decided to practice his new-found kissing skills. She seemed to like the way he did it because she responded eagerly and before he knew it, they were clinched in a passionate embrace and oblivious to pretty much everything else around them.

His head was feeling very fuzzy by the time a second half-naked girl joined them on the cushions and he found himself with more kissing practice than he probably needed. He was aware of Rudolph's presence close by but was a bit preoccupied with hands and mouths and tongues as one of the girls placed her nipple in his mouth, and another ran her hands down the front of his tights.

Bendryn was in heaven with a seemingly endless procession of naked or half-naked bodies to touch and kiss and no end of people wanting to touch him, kiss him, and generally caress him into a whirling state of ecstasy. He remembered having at least one more drink, one with an umbrella in it he thought, and then he vaguely remembered some dancing and perhaps some singing and an awful lot of warm chocolate and gingerbread before the night descended into a blur of lips and nipples and general lust and naughtiness.

At one point he was sure that his girls came and shooed some ponies away and took their places. Pretty sure, at any rate, because he found the kisses warm and familiar and tasting of chocolate and gingerbread. He had shadowy memories of finding himself on his back with both of his girls kissing and touching him like they had done earlier and causing him to get hard, only this time his flashes of memory went quite differently.

From what he could recall, Strawberry knelt over his face while he licked chocolate off her thighs until she lowered her soft wet lips onto his mouth. He had recollections of Miesha's warm breath in his ear. "That's it, Bendryn, kiss her like that. Yes, lick her. She likes that. Press your tongue into her, Bendryn, yes more like that. Harder." Strawberry squirmed on his mouth and made him rock-hard in his tights.

Then Miesha seemed to vanish and Bendryn had brief memories of his tights being pulled down and of his aching hardness being engulfed in a tight warmth that sent him into a spin of ecstasy. He heard cheering and chanting and clapping and after that, his only memory was of swimming in a warm pool of absolute pleasure.

He dreamt of cavorting with mermaids and felt happy and safe and content until his dreams were disturbed by a voice in the distance. He couldn't quite make it out at first. He thought it might have been Sebastian yelling at the girls, but it grew closer and louder and all of a sudden, he was awakened by a very clear call.

"Bendryn Elford! Where the devil is my naughty list?"

Santa! Oh, my God, he's found me.

Bendryn tried to open his eyes but the pounding headache he suddenly became aware of seemed to extend to the tips of his eyelashes and made them too heavy. He attempted to look around him through the smallest of slits, but the room was spinning and he was sure he was going to be sick.

"Bendryn!"

The elf, who's face now almost matched the colour of his clothes, tried to move again but without much luck. He realised his head was resting on Rudolph's flank and they were both surrounded, half covered by naked bodies in various stages of consciousness.

He couldn't move, his head was spinning out of control, and his eyes just wouldn't focus. He was definitely going to be sick.

"Bendryn, Get back here now!" Santa yelled

"Yes, please, beam me up now, Santa," Bendryn groaned and before he barely finished the words, he was on the floor of Santa's office and had a bucket thrust under his face just in time.

Bendryn didn't know what was worse, the heaving or the headache, but once the heaving stopped he decided it was the headache.

He tried to look up at Santa who was standing over him with his hands on his hips, but it hurt too much. He slumped backwards, and his head landed on Rudolph who groaned but showed minimal other life signs.

Then Santa clapped his hands together and the sound was just crushing enough to make both the elf and the reindeer sit up and at least partially open their eyes, so they could try to look blearily at him.

Santa stood over them and looked them up and down, frowning in disgust at the splattering's of jelly, peanut butter, chocolate and goodness knows whatever else. The white powder residue around their noses could have been icing sugar, given the number of gingerbread crumbs they had brought with them. Rudolph had a bra and two pairs of knickers hanging from his antlers, and his nose was flashing intermittently like a neon bulb on its way out.

Bendryn was a sorry sight. His hat was missing, his tunic was askew, and his tights had enormous holes in them showing at least two shades of lipstick all over his buttocks and thighs. One bell was gone completely, and the other was hanging by a thread, and he had a bedraggled looking white stocking hanging out of his pocket.

"Look at you two! You are a disgrace!" Santa said just a little too loudly for Bendryn's head. The smell of them almost curled Santa's eyebrows. "And where the devil is my naughty list?"

Bendryn tried to speak but his tongue seemed to be stuck to the roof of his mouth. Rudolph just shrugged.

"Lucky for you two, I always keep a spare. Goodness knows what you were up to that caused it to self-destruct like that!"

Santa picked up a copy of the naughty list from his desk.

'Phew.' thought Bendryn

Santa opened the list and said, "And who do you suppose is now at the top of the list?"

He turned the list to show them the two top names flashing in bright red with stickers and warnings obscuring, all of the details bar the names: Bendryn Elford and Rudolph Reindeer.

"What were you thinking?" Santa roared.

Both boys shrugged.

"What have you got to say for yourselves?" He roared again.

Bendryn decided he needed to say something if only to stop the roaring.

"Sorry, Santa," he managed rather weakly.

"SORRY? You think sorry even comes close??" Santa roared even louder, causing both boys to wince. "Well you may wince! For crying out loud, my future Third Assistant Sub-Apprentice to the Second Vice-Head of Painting and Construction and my most trusted fog navigating deer steal and destroy the naughty list, run amok in the human world, and return dishevelled, defiled and smelling disgusting and you think SORRY SANTA covers it?"

Bendryn and Rudolph both hung their heads in remorse and could think of nothing to say in their defence.

Santa let them stew there for a while before he finally said, at a slightly lower volume,

"So, what did you learn Bendryn?"

Bendryn looked up and did his best to focus and speak in coherent sentences. "I learned that you can't just walk up to a girl and ask to touch her tits, no matter how naughty she is."

Santa did his best to continue to look stern and not chuckle. "Anything else?" he asked.

"Yes. Never drink anything with an umbrella in it," Bendryn said and then reached for his bucket again.

Once he finished being sick, Bendryn looked up at Santa and noticed he seemed to have less steam coming out of his ears. In fact, he looked rather kindly again.

"I really am truly sorry Santa," he said.

"I know Bendryn," came the kindly reply. "But you do know that you won't be able to take up your post as Third Assistant Sub-Apprentice to the Second Vice-Head of Painting and Construction after this, don't you?"

"Yes, Santa." Bendryn hung his head in sorrow and close to shame.

"However," the old man said. "I may have another position for you. One that I think you will be well suited to."

Santa walked over to his desk and then came back with a set of plans that he showed to Bendryn. Rudolph looked over his shoulder. They were both astounded, and Bendryn was not convinced that he was not dreaming or hallucinating after all.

"What do you think Bendryn?" Santa said. "Are you the elf for the job?"

"Yes sir," he said still a bit bemused. "May I have Rudolph to help me? If he wants to?"

Rudolph and Santa both nodded but then Rudolph looked like he wished he hadn't moved his head so rigorously.

"Very well," said Santa. "Off you two go. Get cleaned up and get some sleep. We will talk more about this when I get back from my rounds. Lucky for you it isn't foggy, Rudolph," Santa chuckled. As he leant down to put the plans back in the drawer, Bendryn decided that he was still way too drunk and definitely hallucinating because for a moment he thought he caught a glimpse of black fishnet stocking as Santa's trousers rode up past the top of his boots a little.

Both the boys took themselves to their homes, got cleaned up, and slept right through the Christmas rush. Bendryn dreamed of his girls, his artist, and her framed artwork and assumed Rudolph dreamt of cavorting ponies, and that might have been the end of the story if not for Santa's plans, which were put into action as soon as the boys were up to the task.

To this day, if you happen to visit the north pole, you would find a building just on the outskirts of Christmas town between the time slip and the reindeer rehab centre. The sign says Bendryn's Bar and Grill, but the locals just call it the cantina. You can't miss it. The flashing neon sign out front alternates between "Jolly Jelly Wrestling" and "Reindeer Games" and if you go in for a drink, you may well be served by one of two tall, slender beauties. Or you might spot a red-nosed reindeer having lunch with some very pretty ponies. And if you're very lucky, you may even be greeted by the happiest naughtiest elf you could ever wish to meet. But you're only allowed upstairs if your name is already on the naughty list.

*****

Kissed by an Angel

Helping my parents decorate the tree was always the highlight of Christmas for me as a kid. Now that I had finished my studies and was home, really home, it felt perfect to be wrestling with tinsel, untangling lights, and trying not to drop the tiny glass baubles under my father's enormous feet.

Finally, it was all but done. I stood back to admire our handy work and my father handed me the Angel we always put on the top.

"Here you go Michael, my boy," Dad said cheerily. "Put your poor old Gabriel up top where he belongs so he can herald in the silly season."

My heart leapt with lingering shadows of boyhood excitement. I remembered when my father used to lift me up to what seemed an impossible height to put the angel in place. Then there were the years of ladders and stepping stools, and now here I was, barely needing to stand on tiptoes to put the finishing touches to our family Christmas tree.

I took the angel carefully and felt a rush of memories. I remembered finding him in a box of religious statues at my preschool fete and insisting to my gran that he was the perfect angel for our tree. She always said she only relented because he reminded her of the covers on her favourite romance novels. The ones with Fabio on them.

He had long blond hair that stood out as if windblown and an extremely well-muscled torso and arms. He held a glitter-encrusted gold trumpet in his outstretched hand and was scantily clad, with just a strategically draped cloth that didn't cover very much. The angel of course, not Fabio.

Gran and I had glued an empty toilet roll to his back. I then painted the cardboard tube with the sort of care and attention to detail last seen in the Sistine Chapel during the early fifteen hundreds. Once the paint dried, my angel Gabriel had become a permanent fixture in our family Christmas tradition.

I reached up and slid the painted toilet roll over the tip of the tree and my parents applauded. I took an exaggerated bow and we all laughed, then headed to the kitchen for a much-needed brunch. As soon as we finished eating, Dad conveniently vanished with a cold beer in hand, saying something about cleaning the BBQ and scooping the leaves out of the pool. Which was secret Dad code for staying out of the way while Mum and I worked our magic in the kitchen, taking it from neat and clean to total Christmas food prep mayhem and back again.

We chopped and rinsed and stuffed and whipped and baked and got through a significant percentage of the cask of white wine in the fridge, some of which even made it into the food. By the time Dad was ready for another beer, we were done and the kitchen was back in order. He shook his head, smiled, and kissed Mum on the head. I knew he was thinking we had over-catered, as usual. Mum just shrugged, wiped her hands on her apron, and hugged him.

The mountain of food would not go astray. We were expecting the whole family for Christmas lunch including my very pregnant sister, her husband, and their four kids, who I loved to bits and hadn't seen for weeks. Apparently, they were bringing the new nanny as well, so with them and the rest of the extended family it was going to be a very full house of hungry people.

After an early-ish dinner, Mum and Dad were heading out to the Christmas Eve service and then to a friend's place to play cards and have 'a couple of Christmas drinks.' They would stay overnight and head back after breakfast. Nobody was due much before lunchtime. So, I had the house to myself for the night. I planned to settle in front of the tele, wild thing that I am, and try to find something worth watching.

As they were leaving Mum went to wipe a spot off my face. I ducked and said, "Mum, I am not nine you know."

"I know," she said. "Why do you think I didn't lick my thumb first?"

The three of us laughed and Mum used the moment of distraction to wipe my face anyway.

"It's glitter," she laughed. "Gold glitter. Who would have thought that old angel would still be shedding glitter after all these years?"

"I know, Edith. It's a Christmas miracle," Dad chuckled and ushered Mum out the door.

Once they were gone, I went and made a big bowl of popcorn and parked myself in front of the TV with the remote control in one hand and a cold white wine in the other.

As it got dark, the lights on the tree switched on and the loungeroom looked like a fairyland. I sat back and just stared at the tree. The flickering lights reflecting off the random bits of gold glitter, made it look like the angel was winking at me. I remembered when I was a kid, I used to talk to the Gabriel statue and imagine he could come to life. The thought made me smile. I winked back at him, grinned at my own silliness, and went back to watching the television, trying not to think about Adrian.

It would be my first Christmas without him since…I couldn't remember when. We had been childhood friends and then high school sweethearts, but about halfway through university we drifted apart. I wanted to study hard, spend time with my family, and be an involved uncle. He wanted the drinking, drugs, and party life. I figured he would settle down after a while, but things came to a head last Christmas when I mentioned marriage and he laughed in my face.

I let it go, but it was over on New Year's Eve when I caught him with another guy at a party. When I freaked out, he told me to grow up and get a life. I tried but I still wasn't sure I had managed either of those things. I had dated but just never found anybody that I clicked with. So here I was, all alone on Christmas Eve and wondering if I would ever meet a guy I could settle down and get a dog with.

Then some old sad movie on the TV tipped me over the edge and I began to cry. Just a few tears at first but it soon progressed into full on sobbing. I don't think I had cried like that for years. I felt desperately sad.

I tried to think of all the positive things in my life. I had great parents, an amazing big sister and brother in law, the best nieces and nephews in the world. I knew I was loved. I was young, fit and healthy, and had nothing to complain about.

But I felt despondent and couldn't help crying like a baby. The weather mirrored my feelings. There was a sudden downpour that turned into a typical Sydney summer storm. My crying was drowned out by the thunder. Then to add to my woes, the power suddenly went out. I probably should have gone to check the fuses, but instead I sat in the silent darkness and wept.

I was wallowing in my self-pity when I heard a deep, strong, man's voice.

"Michael?" it said. "Are you okay Michael?"

"Dad?" I asked, even though it didn't sound anything like my father and I was sure he hadn't come back.

"No, sorry Michael, your father won't be home until tomorrow. But I'm here," the voice replied in a kind tone.

I knew I should have been scared. But I wasn't. Not in the least.

I saw shadowy movement in the near pitch darkness and thought I could make out the figure of a man moving carefully towards me.

"I'm here, Michael," the voice repeated from quite close to me "No need to cry alone," it said from right next to me on the lounge. I felt a strong arm move gently around my shoulders and draw me into a broad chest. "I'm here now Michael," the voice said reassuringly.

I inexplicably burst into further tears and blubbed almost inconsolably in the arms of an unknown phantom stranger in my darkened house on Christmas Eve.

"Shh now," the voice said while rocking me like a baby. "Hush now. No need for tears. Tell me what's troubling you so."

For the longest time I couldn't speak at all. Then when I could, I wasn't very coherent.

I sat up a little and tried to pull myself together.

"I don't have a lover," I said, as much to myself as to the phantom.

"Really?" the voice said with the hint of a chuckle.

I pulled back and tried to make out who it was in the dark but couldn't.

"Yes, really," I said feeling a little tetchy.

"Relax Michael," the phantom said, and I felt his hand brush the hair out of my eyes. "I don't have a lover either. But I think I know where I can find one."

He touched my cheek with his large hand and kissed me tenderly. It was just a brush on the lips for the briefest of moments, but my heart went into overdrive and started flipping around like a stranded sardine.

"Who are you?" I managed to ask

He chuckled "You know who I am Michael. I'm your Gabriel. Come to finally be with you, for tonight at least. Now I'd like to kiss you properly if I may."

"My Gabriel?" I asked. "My angel Gabriel?"

"Yes, Michael, your angel Gabriel. Now may I kiss you? I have waited a long time."

I didn't doubt what he was saying for a moment. I believed him. As crazy as it sounds, I believed he was my Gabriel. Although that could have been because I just drunk too much wine and would wake up any moment to realise I was dreaming. But I didn't want to wake up yet. Not yet.

"May I kiss you properly, Michael?" The voice came out of the darkness, rich and warm and with a tone of infinite patience.

It dawned on me that I hadn't answered him.

"Yes," I finally responded, hoping I would get through the whole kiss before I woke up and regained my senses.

He put his big strong hand gently on my face again. His fingertips slid smoothly through my hair as he cupped my head and drew my mouth to his. He pressed his lips to mine and kissed me more thoroughly. My heart fluttered as he kissed just my bottom lip, sucking it gently, then the top lip on its own. His lips were soft and the hint of stubble on his face sent a major surge of desire through me.

He put his other hand up, ran his fingers through my hair then held my head in both of his powerful hands and kissed me. He teased the tip of his tongue along my lips then kissed me deeply, pressing his tongue into my eager mouth and making contact with mine.

I felt myself melt into him completely. I didn't care if he was a phantom, an apparition, a dream, or whatever he was. I just let myself sink into the moment. Into him.

I tentatively put my hand up to touch him. Aching to feel his body but afraid he would vanish if I moved too fast. He didn't. I rested my palm on his broad chest and could feel his hard muscles under his smooth skin. I almost swooned at the feel of him. Hard, strong, perfect.

I responded to his kisses in earnest, exploring his sweet, warm mouth with my tongue. He tasted good, he smelled good, and he felt like absolute perfection. The sound of his breathing made my heart beat harder. I'd never had a dream so real and I prayed it would last the whole night through.

The kissing became almost frantic, urgent and frenetic, and our hands were all over each other. Touching, exploring, enjoying.

Gabriel, or whoever he was, kissed my neck and throat just exactly the way I liked and I realised I had an aching need pressing itself hard on the inside of my underwear, doing its best to break out of my jeans.

He kissed his way up to my ear and whispered eagerly, "Could we possibly go upstairs, Michael?"

"Yes, yes," I said with maybe a bit too much enthusiasm.

He chuckled and stood up. I could see him a little more with the moonlight coming through the window and my heart almost skipped a beat at how much he reminded me of my romance cover angel. I stood, and he took my hand. Just as I was about to lead him up to my room, I remembered the power was out.

"I really should check the circuit board," I said reluctantly "I don't want all the food to spoil if it is just a fuse."

"Relax Michael," he said. "I will take care of it." And with that, he raised his free hand and sort of waved it over his shoulder. The Christmas lights came back on and I could hear the faint purr of the fridge coming from the kitchen. I relaxed. My shadowy companion then scooped me up into his big strong arms and carried me up to my room as if I were no more than a doll.

He stood me in the middle of my bedroom floor and kissed me. The feeling of his mouth on mine causing my erection to strain even harder against its constraints. He put his enormous arms around me and pulled me close to him so that I was now pressing my hardness up against his thigh. If he wasn't aware of what he was doing to me before, that surely left him no doubt.

"I'd like to undress you, Michael," he whispered softly in my ear.

I nodded, then feared he may not see me in the darkness so said, "Yes," out loud.

He effortlessly undid the buttons of my shirt and moved on to the jeans buttons without pause. He slid my shirt off my shoulders and it dropped to the floor. He pushed my jeans down past my thighs and let them fall the rest of the way. Before I even had a chance to wonder what the hell I was doing, I was standing in front of him in just my boxer shorts.

A sudden flash of lightning illuminated the room just long enough for me to see our reflection in my bedroom mirror. He looked exactly like my tree angel, my Gabriel, and was even wearing the same scanty robe. I figured this had to be a dream and one I didn't want to wake from before I had done what I wanted. I felt a rush of urgency and reached up to his shoulder, sliding the fabric off. It fell as far as his waist, then I realised he was wearing some sort of sash. I fumbled with it in the dark until I finally got it undone, and to my immense pleasure the whole garment fell to the floor.

He drew me to him, held our bodies hard against one another, and kissed me. I felt his passion all the way to my soul and thought I might faint. I could feel his erection pressing into me now and I realised he was naked.

I wasn't sure what came over me, but I had to have him, right then and there before I had a chance to wake up. I dropped to my knees and took him into my mouth. I felt him groan as I slid my lips over the smooth hard head of his cock and took as much of him into my mouth as I could. I began to suck him the way I hoped he liked it and I felt his hands on my head as if to reassure me that he did.

He felt good in my mouth, smooth and hard. I teased the head with the tip of my tongue and felt him groan again as I tasted a hint of his saltiness. I ached to taste more, to taste and swallow all of him.

I heard his voice as if in the distance as his fingertips raked through my hair. "We don't need to rush this, Michael, we have all night."

I did hear him, but I was not stopping for anything. I had never had a man like him before, real or imagined, and I was not letting him get away until I had felt him come at least once.

I kept my mouth firmly around his beautiful cock and began running my hands over every inch of him that I could reach. His thighs were like tree trunks, hard and unyielding. I could feel every muscle, strong and defined, and it made my knees go weak. His belly was taut with a perfect treasure trail leading from his navel to the course patch of hair I had my face practically buried in. I slid my hands up higher and ran my fingers over a solid wall of abs. I felt my erection twitch and my balls ache at the feel of the corrugations. He was like a whole body of sexy braille and I wanted to read every word.

I moved my hands around behind him and slid across his smooth, perfectly rounded butt. The thrill that ran through me was worthy of a Vivaldi concerto and it made me shiver from head to toe.

I felt him moan and grip my hair. I knew I was about to get what I wanted. Him.

"If you don't want me to spill in your mouth, Michael, you had better stop now," I heard him struggle to say.

I dug my fingers into his butt cheeks and pushed as hard as I could to keep him in my mouth, hoping that was an obvious enough signal that I wanted to taste his every last drop. He let out a deep growling rumble and gripped my hair tightly. I used every skill I had, taking him deep into my mouth, then sliding out enough to get my tongue working all the most sensitive parts of his head, then sucking him in deep again.

He began moving his hands strongly with the rhythm of my movement and showed me what he liked. I moved with him, savouring every inch of him and every delicious preview of his saltiness on my tongue. I was in heaven. He changed tack on me, holding my head still in his firm grip and moving himself in and out of my mouth. I could feel the tension in him rising and I prayed desperately to Eros, Priapus, or any other deity that might listen that I would not wake up before I felt the warm result of his climax in my mouth and down my throat.

His buttocks clenched, and he held my head tight, pressing deep into my throat. The anticipation was exquisite as we both held still, frozen on the cusp of resolution for the briefest of moments. The perfectly still silence was finally broken by the rumbling groan escaping his lips as he began to fill my eager mouth with pulsing surges of his ejaculation.

I swallowed him, all of him, down to the last drop that escaped from him and then sighed with deep satisfaction as he loosened his grip on my head and lifted me to my feet. I was a little shaky, but he held me tenderly against his hard body until I was steady. I pressed my head to his chest and could feel he was panting still, his heart was beating hard and fast.

'I did that to you,' I thought to myself and grinned a little.

He kissed the top of my head as if he heard my thought. My grin turned to a full smile. He kissed my forehead, my face, my neck. By the time he finally moved to my mouth, I was so hungry for him I moaned with sheer relief. He started slow and gentle but soon the furious urgency returned, at least on my part. I couldn't get enough of him. I kissed and bit and sucked his tongue into my mouth and he responded, matching my burning lust with a demanding passion of his own.

I felt his large hands running down my back. He slipped his fingers under the elastic of my boxers and slid his hands in, cupping my naked flesh in his palms. I shivered but didn't take my mouth off his. He slid my underwear down far enough that I could wiggle it the rest of the way and step out of it, then he pressed my naked body to his. Just as I feared my cock might explode, he grabbed a fistful of my hair and pulled my head to the side. He kissed my neck then growled in my ear.

"I need to have you in my mouth now, Michael, please."

His urgency spread through me like a grass fire, so I took his hand and led him the few steps to my bed. The lightning flashed outside again, and I caught another glimpse of him. Dream, apparition, phantom, whatever he was - he was built like a god and I planned to enjoy as much of him as I could before he disappeared.

He laid me gently on the bed. He kissed my lips, my neck, my chest. He paused to gently suck each of my nipples into his mouth and tease them until they were hard. I desperately wanted him to get where he was going but I didn't want him to rush. It took me all my will to relax and enjoy the feeling of his warm lips and gently probing tongue on my skin, as he worked his way down my now trembling body.

When he dipped his tongue into my navel, it sent a spark of urgent heat directly to my balls and my hand went automatically to the back of his head as if to push him to where I wanted him to be. I felt him chuckle softly and whisper.

"Patience, Michael, I will not leave you before dawn. Trust me."

I felt oddly reassured. Even though I was sure I was dreaming, part of me had fully bought into the idea that he was my Gabriel, come to life, and I trusted him. Completely.

I relaxed and let him linger, slowly working his way to my impatient yearning cock. When he by-passed it and kissed his way down my thigh, I thought I might die, but he rested one hand on my belly as if to quell my impatience while he kissed and licked his way down one leg and back up the other. When I finally felt his warm breath on my balls, I almost cried with relief. He kissed them gently and teased them a little with his lips. When he cupped them in his hand and ran his tongue up my shaft, I was sure I was going to come in about two seconds flat.

He swirled his wet tongue around the head of my aching cock, seeking out my most private areas of pleasure and expertly exploiting each one he found. I laid back and closed my eyes so that I could concentrate on the feeling of what he was doing to me.

When I felt him take me into his mouth, I groaned and had to work hard not to come right then. He held still, obviously aware of my plight, and gave me time to regain some level of control. Then he expertly worked my cock with his warm wet mouth, backing off each time I got too close to climaxing. Making me ache, making me whimper, making my legs tremble, and finally making me beg.

"Please, now, let me come now, please," I implored, sure I could feel him smile at how easily he had subjugated me, but I didn't care in the least. I just needed him to let me orgasm more than I ever needed anything before in my life.

He let me build again and this time I knew he was going to take me the whole way. I relaxed and let him take charge of my growing need. I felt it, like a herd of runaway horses galloping towards me, until I got to that point where I knew nothing would stop it now.

My back arched and every cell of my body tensed in anticipation of what was about to happen. I was held there for barely a heartbeat and then I heard myself cry out as the horses galloped over me, pummeling me into insensibility with the most intense pleasure I had ever felt.

I felt myself spilling my load into his warm wet mouth and I knew he was swallowing all I had to offer. But my mind was lost on some other plane and I wasn't sure I ever wanted to come back.

I was aware, on some level, of my phantom lover moving up onto the bed beside me and wrapping me in his arms. I felt warm and safe and happy. I rested my head comfortably on his chest and let myself bask in the afterglow for a while. I found myself absentmindedly running my fingertips along the outline of his abs and marvelling at how perfect his body was.

The streetlight outside my room took the edge off the darkness and I could see at least the shadowy form of my mystery man, my lover, my angel. I looked up and tried to see his face clearly, but it was still too dark for that.

"Will you really stay until dawn?" I asked running a fingertip across his chest and marvelling at his pecs.

"Yes, Michael. I will be here until dawn, and then I have to go."

"Will you come back?" I asked.

"Not like this," he said. "I can't come back like this again." He rolled on to his side and kissed my forehead. "Much as I would like to."

"Can you not just stay with me?" I knew the answer, but I posed the question anyway.

"No, Michael. There are rules and limits, and I have already broken several of them just to be with you tonight."

"Why?" I asked.

"Because I love you, Michael. I have always loved you."

I had the feeling that there was more to that answer than I could possibly understand but it comforted me.

"Would you stay if you could?" I pressed

"Would you want me to stay?" he replied

"Yes, yes of course," I said. "I would give anything for you to stay." I had no idea why I felt so attached to what was probably a dream but I did, and I went with it.

He sighed, a long almost despairing sigh that all but broke my heart. He kissed my lips tenderly then laid back on the bed beside me with his hand up behind his head as if he was deep in thought. I pressed my body against him and was comforted by his warmth.

I kissed his chest and flicked his nipple with my tongue. He groaned. I gently sucked the nipple into my mouth and teased it with the tip of my tongue then bit it softly as it stiffened. He put his hand on my head and ran his fingers through my hair.

"You make it difficult to think when you do that, Michael," he chuckled

"I wasn't aiming for deep thought," I replied a little cheekily

He laughed. "You always were incorrigible," he said and tousled my hair.

"Then kiss me," I teased.

He obliged without hesitation. His mouth was warm and sweet, and his stubble grazed my lips just the way I liked it.

It started slow and tender but soon heated up to the sort of feverish kissing guaranteed to get me hard, which it did. Soon we were lying on our sides, kissing wildly, with both our second erections pressed between us. His passion and hunger inflamed my own, and soon we were in danger of combusting.

"I need you, Michael," he growled in my ear

I felt a sudden panic. I feared that my eagerness had let him think I might go further than I was prepared to go, and I felt very self-conscious, but I needed to speak up.

"I...I, umm... I don't," I stammered uselessly

He put a finger to my lips.

"Shh, Michael. I know you don't and that wasn't what I meant. It's okay."

I felt relieved but still wanted to try to explain myself.

"It isn't that I wouldn't want you to... umm... you know," I barely managed to say before I felt self-conscious and shy and awkward.

"It is okay, Michael, I understand," he said in that patient tone. But I wanted to finish.

I took a deep breath and said, "I'm saving myself." It suddenly felt stupid when I said it out loud, but I pressed on. "I want to wait until I get married. I always fancied being married in white."

I feared he would laugh at me but instead, he put one hand behind my neck and kissed me with such tenderness I almost started to cry again.

"I know Michael, and that is beautiful, but it wasn't what I meant"

I didn't let him finish for fear he really would make me cry and spoil the rest of the night. I kissed him hard and deep and pressed my body against him.

He groaned and responded by reaching down between us and taking both our cocks in his one large hand. I gasped at how good that felt.

"Are you okay?" he asked.

I nodded and smiled, feeling a little shy but eager.

He continued and began to play with us both like we were one, pressing us together and rubbing his thumb over the slippery, glistening heads until we were slick with each other's wetness.

The kissing became electric and I could barely breathe. I felt like we had become a single entity, held together in his hand. I could feel the passion rising in both of us at an almost alarming rate and I had a momentary panic when I feared I might wake up too soon.

I felt myself break into a sweat, not sure if it was from fear, passion, or the hot summer night. I struggled to keep kissing him. His hand was still on the back of my neck and we ended up with our foreheads pressed together, panting and sweating as he expertly jerked us both off at the same time.

I closed my eyes, almost overwhelmed by the pleasure and the urgency, and let myself just feel. Feel the pressure of his hardness pressed against mine in his powerful grip. I could hear from his breathing that he was building with me, stroke for stroke, and I hoped I could last long enough to climax with him. Or at least not too much before. I could hear grunting, almost like a wild animal, but couldn't tell who was making the noise. Maybe both of us.

His movement became hard and fast and frantic, and I was lost in it. I couldn't do anything but merely hold on for the ride and try not to come too soon. I felt myself getting to the point of no return and attempted to tell him, but I couldn't speak. I stopped trying. I let go and left myself in his hands, literally.

He gripped the back of my neck tightly, his palm sweating - or was that me? He held my face to his, our mouths close but not touching, each of us panting heavily and lost in our own pressing need. I felt pressure building in my groin and I knew I was going to explode. His panting increased as did the sound of groaning and grunting. I felt, rather than heard, a deep rumble in him, emanating from low in his belly and travelling up his torso. When it reached his mouth and he cried out, I was startled at first and then I realised he was climaxing before me.

The thought of that, the sound of him still ringing in my ears and the smell of our sweat, combined to push me over the edge and I heard my own groans just seconds behind his. Almost instantaneously I was adding to the warm sticky mess that was spilling out onto his hand and spreading over our skin. The thought of my come on those perfect abs sent a shudder through me and made even my receding erection twitch.

We were largely stilled and quiet. Our foreheads still pressed together as we tried to catch our collective breath. The only movement was the rise and fall of our chests. I didn't want to move, but I reached behind myself to where I knew there was a towel and handed it to him. He took it and cleaned us both up, then laid on his back and pulled me on top of him.

He kissed me so tenderly and lovingly I wept. I couldn't help it, it just happened. He didn't try to stop me he just held me and kissed me and rocked me until I finished, then he lay me down beside him with his strong arm around my shoulders and I rested my head on his chest. I lazily traced the muscles of his stomach and played with the hairs below his navel. Then I recalled something he had said.

"What did you mean?" I asked.

He chuckled. "You may need to give me another clue, Michael."

"Sorry," I said, realising that was a bit vague. "Before, when you said you needed me. If you didn't mean what I assumed you meant. What did you mean?"

"I meant I need you, Michael, I need to be with you. I'd like to be the one you're saving yourself for, if you would have me."

"Of course, I would have you," I responded. "I'd have you in a flash, but I didn't think it was possible." I felt a spark of hope despite not being certain this was real.

"It isn't possible," he started, and my hope was dashed. He obviously sensed my disappointment, but he continued to speak. "It isn't possible like this, Michael, I can't be with you like this past the dawn. But there may be a way."

I sat up and tried to see his face in the darkness, but I couldn't make out his expression.

"How?" I asked eagerly

"Well, it can be tricky," he replied. "I could choose to become mortal for you, Michael, but it has its problems and it could all end very badly for me."

"Tell me what I would need to do, I'll do anything," I said almost ranting and suddenly filled with an awful fear that the dawn would come before we were done. He took a deep breath and sighed.

"The problem would be that as a mortal, I would have no memory of this - of us, of who I am - and if you don't find me, I will be stranded in a mortal body for the duration of a human life with no knowledge of why I'm here. And if you do find me, you can never tell me who I am or remind me of our night together. It is far too hard for an angel to survive knowing that, even if you could convince me of it. It would be up to you to find me and let me fall in love with you in a human way." He looked desperately sad as if he was afraid of what I was about to say.

Part of me just wanted to jump in feet first and insist he stay with me, but I took a moment before I asked, "If you live a whole human life, do you then die when your human self dies or do you go back to being an Angel and get your memories back?"

He smiled as if I had asked just the right question.

"When my human body died, my angel soul would be released, with all my memories intact, as well as the memories of my human existence." He cupped my cheek in his hand and ran his thumb across my brow.

"So, you would be safe and okay?" I was seeking confirmation.

"Yes, Michael, I would be safe and okay. But if you didn't find me, I would always have a sense of loss and not belonging that I didn't understand."

"That would be awful," I said. "How will I find you?"

"You ask that as if it is a done deal," he said with a chuckle

"Isn't it?" I asked

He was silent for a painfully long time and I really had to fight the urge to speak, but I managed to give him the time he needed.

"Yes, Michael," he said. "Yes, it is a done deal if you will have me and take care of me."

"Yes, yes of course," I said. "How will I know where to find you?"

"That is the tricky part," he said. "I can come into your life at any point in your timeline and you may not recognise me in my human form. I will be just like you, Michael," he said with what sounded like an amused tone.

"What if you get here in my past?" I asked, suddenly afraid. "I might not even know to look for you."

He looked a bit pensive, then said, "I'm sure I can work it so that our paths cross in your future, so that should be okay."

"How will I recognise you? Will you look like you?"

"What do I look like, Michael?" he asked in a serious tone

I realised then that I couldn't see him clearly enough to describe him. I felt deflated.

"Mortal humans can't really see us clearly, we are always a bit shadowy and unclear in their memories, but I have an idea," he said. "Kiss my belly, Michael."

I bent to place a kiss on his belly just below and to the side of his navel. As my lips touched his skin, he flinched and a searing heat forced me to draw back. When I looked, there was the imprint of my kiss gently glowing on his belly.

"The mark will be there always, Michael; you will know it's me when you see it."

"Will all my kisses burn you?" I asked

"No Michael, just that one. The rest are safe," he said with a warm chuckle.

"Good," I said. "I'd better take advantage of this body while you still have it."

Then I kissed his belly again and began kissing him all over. I worked my way methodically over every muscle, every sinew. I ran my tongue along every prominent vein and in every rise and fall of his abs, his chest, his thighs. I got him to roll over, so I could revel in the glory that was his perfectly muscled back. When I got him to roll back, I started at his mouth and worked my way down his body, kissing and nibbling at his nipples then moving my way down his treasure trail to the main prize.

I took his semi-hard cock into my mouth and revived it until it filled my mouth perfectly, then began to give him the best head I had ever given anybody in my life.

He maneuvered us so that he could get his mouth around my hard-on and we spent most of the rest of the night slowly pleasuring each other in every way we could think of, short of what we were saving for the wedding night. I had no doubt it was real. I had no doubt I would find him and no doubt we would live out our lives together happily.

The urgency was gone, the fear was gone, and as the dawn was coming closer, he held me tightly and said, "I love you, Michael, I have always loved you. Look out for me. I will need you to find me."

Then he kissed me tenderly, and I fell asleep.

I didn't feel him go but when I woke up, I was alone. I took a little while to get my bearings, and when I did, I smiled at the memory of my hot sex dream. The details were a bit sketchy and fading fast, but I knew I had enjoyed it. I showered and dressed. My parents would be home soon and then the guests would be arriving.

As I worked my way through my morning, everything I touched seemed to be sprinkled with gold glitter and I wondered if I had handled the tree angel that much before I went to bed. I couldn't remember doing it. When I looked at the tree, it all seemed a bit duller and less sparkly. Maybe because it was daylight and the lights weren't on.

My parents got home as I was having breakfast. Mum was astounded that the fridge stayed on and the food was all fine.

"The rest of the street was without power all night," she said. "I heard it on the news. I can't believe ours was okay."

"It's a Christmas miracle, Edith" Dad said, winking at me.

"Well that is two miracles then" Mum replied. "And you know these things happen in threes."

"Well maybe we'll win the lottery next," Dad said, his usual response to Mum's superstitions.

The guests started arriving in dribs and drabs. Dad fired up the barbeque. Mum and I started laying out the rest of the food. I was eager to see my sister and the kids so when I saw her car pull up, I wiped my hands and headed for the door. I was almost bowled over by exuberant children wanting to tell me all about what Santa had brought them, but their father ushered them inside and I helped my sister up the stairs. I hugged her over her baby belly and she pointed back towards the van.

"The nanny is bringing the baby and Mika is still in her seat. She wants her Uncle Michael."

I dutifully headed to the van and saw slim hips and a pert backside nicely filling a pair of well-fitted jeans. The owner was leaning into the back of the van to get the baby bag and goodness knows what else. I quickly checked out a bit more of what I assumed was the nanny. Neat sandals, snuggly fitting t-shirt, honey blonde hair pulled back into a casual bun. Then Mika, the four-year-old, noticed me and launched herself into my arms.

"Uncle Michael!" she squealed with childish delight and the nanny stood up. He took a step towards me with Aiden, the ten-month-old, on his hip and held out a hand for me to shake.

I took it and he smiled.

"You must be Michael," he said as he shook my hand. "I'm Gabe. The kids have told me all about you." He was gorgeous, totally gorgeous, and his smile seemed to light up the whole street. Something in the back of my mind was trying to get my attention, but I couldn't quite grasp it.

Gabe put the baby bag over his shoulder and his shirt rode up a little just as Aiden pushed his foot down on the top of Gabe's jeans, exposing more of his belly. I saw it then, a birthmark in the shape of a perfect set of lips.

My whole night flooded back to me in sharper clarity than I could have previously imagined, and I almost got a hard-on. I must have been staring because Gabe motioned to the birthmark and said, "Mum always said I must have been kissed by an Angel."

I gathered myself together as best as I could and led him into the house.

As I passed the tree, I winked at the now lifeless statue and grinned widely to myself as I thought 'Christmas miracles do come in threes after all.'

*****

The Perfect Gift

Rebecca leant on the counter and watched as the young male shop assistant stood outstretched atop a ladder, endeavouring to retrieve the last pink tricycle in the whole store from its display position, suspended from the ceiling close to the top of the giant tree.

His lean, outstretched body was taut, and every muscle was working as he strained to reach the bike, unhook it, and maintain his balance at the same time. It was a beautiful sight and for the first time, Rebecca was grateful for the stupid, body-hugging elf costumes they had to wear this year.

She sighed. She could think of nothing nicer than the sight of a tight green shirt riding up to reveal unexpectedly lovely abs, a flat toned belly, and just the right amount of treasure trail leading down to snugly fitting green shorts that gave way to green tights clinging to well-muscled thighs.

"You know you could lose your job for ogling the staff like that." She was startled by the voice from behind her breaking into her reverie.

She turned to face the man behind her, "Well, yes possibly," she said. "But not if I'm caught by the man I saw eyeing off the same delicious body and practically drooling, not half an hour ago."

Bryce laughed and leant on the counter beside her.

"You may have a point there, sweet cheeks," he replied as they recommenced watching the aerial ballet. "But I think he might be batting for my team."

"I'm fine with look but not touch," she replied. "And you think every good-looking man is batting for your team." She pressed her shoulder into him as a teasing nudge.

"I can't help it if the world looks prettier and more glittery through my rainbow coloured glasses. Now, aren't you glad I insisted on the tighter fitting costumes this year?"

"Mmm," Rebecca said. "Wish I had popcorn, this is better than a movie."

"Looks like we aren't the only ones appreciating the view." Bryce nudged Rebecca and gestured towards the other young man standing at the bottom of the ladder waiting to take the tricycle once it was freed from its bonds.

He was dressed the same but in red and was facing away from them, giving a great view of a cute tush in skin-tight shorts and red tights clinging to a pair of very nice legs, which were shown off to great effect as he stood up on his toes to reach the prized pink cycle as it was handed down.

"Nice arms on that one, too," she mumbled as a customer approached the counter with a trolley full of toys.

"Well maybe if I dress in yellow, I can get in between them, and we can play traffic lights," Bryce mumbled back with a cheeky grin.

"You're an incorrigible floozy," Rebecca said and then turned with her best beaming smile, ready to serve the customer.

Rebecca had been helping out in her grandfather's toy shop during the Christmas rush ever since she could remember. She used to have a special stool behind the counter so that she could reach the till.

This was the first time she had worked there since her cousin Bryce had taken over the day to day running of the shop after their Grandad's stroke forced him to give up full-time work.

There had been a few changes. New shelving and a coat of paint mostly, and for the Christmas season a much bigger tree with an impressive toy display. There was also a new 'Christmas Castle Cubby' fitted out with bean bags and cushions for the kids to play in while their parents shopped. It was the largest of the cubbies they stocked, big enough for adults to easily get in and out of, so you could fit a lot of kids in there and they seemed to love it. However, Bryce told Rebecca he was rethinking it after more than a couple of parents had left their kids to 'nap' in there while they went over to the cafe across the road for lunch.

The new costumes were also Bryce's doing. It had been a tradition for the staff to dress up as Santa's elves and for Grandad to dress up as Santa in the week prior to Christmas. Bryce continued the tradition but wanted to bring it up to date a bit.

He looked more like Santa's hot grandson than the Jolly old elf their grandfather had been. Rebecca was subjected to the indignity of red sequined bib and brace hot pants with green tights, red shoes, and a green and red striped t-shirt that was so tight she had to go out and buy a special t-shirt bra to wear under it, so she was not showing her nipples through her clothes.

"Spoilsport," Bryce had said when she came back from the lingerie shop looking smooth and demure. "How am I going to attract all those young fathers into the shop now?" he complained with a wink.

"Hmm, let me see," Rebecca said with her finger exaggeratedly on her chin. "Maybe by selling toys rather than exploiting the breasts of your hapless cousin perhaps?"

"Novel idea," he had said and kissed her on the forehead.

There was only a couple of years age difference between them and they had grown up more like siblings than anything else, which was great for Rebecca who loved being an only child but still got to have a pseudo big brother when she needed him. She would also class Bryce as her best friend, better than her best girlfriends. They talked about everything and had no secrets, nothing was considered too much information or too trivial or too serious. They knew each other's lives inside out and spent time together as often as possible. So, working with him on Christmas Eve was no hardship at all. In fact, Rebecca loved it.

Rebecca never understood why people left so much of their toy shopping until so late; it wasn't as if Christmas happened unexpectedly. But every year there was that frantic last-minute dash for that special must have thing and it seemed to be worse in the years since the shop started staying open until midnight.

So, from about five in the afternoon until about eleven, they were super busy. Thank God the Santa photos had been outsourced now and were no longer their responsibility.

Rebecca, Bryce, Luke (the green elf) and Ryan (the red elf) were all serving customers while about half a dozen other staff were scurrying about, helping people find things, carrying parcels out to cars, putting stuff back on shelves, and digging out laybys. They were one of a few remaining old-fashioned sort of stores that still did layby, but only for big-ticket items and only for Christmas. They were meant to be picked up by nine pm, but there were still trampolines and swing sets going out the back door to the loading bay when things were beginning to wind down at eleven.

"Somebody is going to have a very late night," Bryce commented to Rebecca as a build-it-yourself cubby, a small above ground pool, and complete gym set were being loaded into the back of a van and squeezed between several kids' booster seats.

Rebecca nodded and leant back on Bryce, who put his arms around her and hugged her.

"Thanks for your help tonight Bec. I'd have been lost without you. Are you still okay to stay and lock up for me if I dash off shortly?"

"Sure, cuz," she said with a smile. "When are you going to bring him to a family do?"

Bryce sighed. "It is still early days lovely, but maybe soon. I think he is the forever one Bec, but I don't want to jinx it. We have an appointment next week, just to check we are all safe." He put "safe" in inverted air commas and winked.

"Oh my god, Bryce!" she exclaimed. "Do I hear monogamy on its way?"

"Yes, honey," he responded. "And who knows what after that?"

Rebecca hugged her cousin. She so wanted him to be happy.

"Are you all okay with your tests and stuff?" he asked suddenly more serious than usual.

"Yep, I'm all fine," Rebecca said and put her hand up for a high five. Bryce responded with a high five, which morphed into a complex series of moves ending in a silly handshake and they laughed. They had been working on that since she was three.

"Oh, and I've not bought your pressie yet, gorgeous. I looked at a few things, but nothing screamed 'the perfect gift' at me," Bryce said. "But if all else fails we can go shopping and have a girlie day together next week, leave the boys in charge while it's quiet." He gestured towards Luke and Ryan who were tidying up some of the extreme chaos that was a toy shop on Christmas Eve. "How does that sound?"

"Perfect," she said. "Now you get your cute keister out of here and leave us to it. I think the rush has passed and you look bushed. I'll see you at Grandma and Grandpa's tomorrow. Give my love to Jeremy."

Bryce headed off and Rebecca started letting the other staff go in dribs and drabs as they finished their tasks.

By closing time, there was only Luke and Ryan left. Both said they would hang around and do a bit more tidying while she counted the takings and balanced the till and would then help her lock up and walk her to her car. She didn't really feel like she needed protecting but it was nice of them to offer and there was no harm in having two gorgeous guys walk her out, even if they do fancy each other, she thought.

She found she got through sorting and bagging the cash much faster than anticipated - one of the joys of most people paying by card. She locked the money in the office safe, gathered up her gear, and went looking for the boys before she set the alarm.

She couldn't see them anywhere and she hated calling out in a quiet building at this hour of the night, so she went looking for them instead. As she passed the Christmas Castle Cubby, she was sure she heard a muffled sound, and for a dreadful moment she wondered if somebody had left their child behind.

She stepped inside. She hadn't been in there before. It was quite cosy, lots of cushions and some little bean bags, and a big bundle of paper fastened to the wall with a bucket of crayons below it on a string. The cubby was an L shape, and once again she thought she heard a sound, so she stepped around the corner with no idea what she might find.

Luke was on his back on a pile of cushions, naked from the waist down, and Ryan was on his knees with Luke's cock in his mouth. Rebecca froze, not sure what the hell to do. She decided the best thing was to go back out as quietly as possible then make some noise outside as if she was looking for them and hope that would be enough to bring them out. But despite her decision, she was still frozen. Her feet wouldn't move, and her eyes were glued to what she was seeing.

She had never seen anything quite so hot, and she felt her body responding much faster than she would have expected. The sight of Luke's erection vanishing repeatedly between Ryan's lips was making her instantly horny and she didn't want to stop watching. Her desire to stay and watch was being matched by her fear of being caught, but before she could take any action either way, Luke looked right at her.

Her heart leapt straight to her throat and she wondered if there was still time to back away discretely, although she knew there wasn't. She was paralysed in her panic until Luke smiled at her and held out his hand as if inviting her to come closer. She was almost tempted to look over her shoulder to check he meant her. But she was still too frozen for even that.

Luke kept his hand outstretched and beckoned. Rebecca knew for sure he was inviting her over to them, but she was still unsure what to do. She liked what she was seeing but she was also totally confronted by the situation.

She stayed where she was, watching Ryan sucking Luke's cock like an expert.

"Please, Rebecca," Luke said, and beckoned again. "We were hoping you would join us."

Rebecca was astounded at how casual and relaxed he seemed, given the circumstances, and was further thrown when Ryan looked up at her and winked.

Rebecca wondered if she had been drawn into some parallel universe where this situation was as normal as walking in on your co-workers having a tea break and being invited to join them for a cuppa.

She had only known them since she'd been popping in to help Bryce, now that uni was finished for the year. Luke and Ryan had been working there on weekends and in their uni breaks all year, so they had been very friendly and helpful bringing her up to speed with the recent changes, and she got on well with them. But this was blowing her mind.

Luke gestured more insistently and smiled so beautifully that Rebecca felt she had nothing to lose. They were both really hot guys, she was single, and they were all adults, so why not relax and see what sort of fun she might have? She figured this was one of those moments where she might regret it for the rest of her life if she didn't take the chance.

She took a tentative step forward, and the wattage of Luke's smile went off the scale. Rebecca carefully drew closer and held out her own hand towards Luke's. As soon as their fingers met, a bolt of pleasure flashed through Rebecca and she knew she would not back out now.

Luke's fingers were strong but smooth and gentle, and as soon as Rebecca was close enough, he took her hand and guided her down beside him.

He took her bag off her shoulder and placed it out of the way, above his head, next to what Rebecca now realised were his tights, shorts and shoes. She noticed that Ryan had backed off a little and was just kissing and teasing the head of Luke's cock as if giving him some time to get her settled.

Before she had much more time to think, she was laying on the makeshift bed of cushions, beside the half-naked Luke, and he was cupping her face in his hands and kissing her. His lips were warm and soft, and his mouth tasted sweet and just slightly of coffee and chocolate. She kissed him back. She hadn't been kissed for months and it felt tremendous. As Luke's tongue explored her mouth, she remembered that while he was in her mouth, his cock was in Ryan's and she felt a rush of warmth between her legs.

The sensual warmth of Luke's kisses began to build to a burning hunger that took Rebecca's breath away. She noticed Ryan was working Luke's cock with an expert mouth and she was sure Luke was about to climax. His kisses became furious, almost frenzied, and Rebecca eagerly kept pace with the frantic lips and tongue until Luke filled her mouth with the sound of his orgasm and she knew he was filling Ryan's mouth with something other than sensuous moans.

It was after midnight on Christmas Eve in a children's toy shop cubby house, and Rebecca thought she had just had the hottest sexual experience of her life... and she still had her clothes on.

Luke's kisses didn't stop, but they changed to a smooth, slow, sensual exploration of Rebecca's mouth and tongue. She didn't realise she had her eyes closed until she opened them to see Ryan climbing up beside Luke.

Luke shifted to put one arm around Rebecca's shoulders and one arm around Ryan's. He then guided them together until their lips touched and Rebecca found herself eagerly kissing her second man for the day. Ryan's mouth was equally warm and welcoming. He tasted sweet and minty, like the red and white striped candy canes they had on the shop counter for the "good" children. As their kiss grew deeper and her tongue probed his mouth, she could sense the lingering salty taste of Luke, and she felt a rush of blood to all parts south.

Luke moved his hands to the backs of their heads and drew them both down to his mouth. To Rebecca's amazement, he joined the kiss. Rebecca had never even considered that she could kiss two men at the same time and yet here she was with two hot sensual mouths on hers and two delicious probing tongues exploring her lips, her teeth, her tongue. She could tell who was who by the slight difference in their taste and she noticed Ryan's stubble was slightly more apparent than Luke's but she didn't really care who she was kissing at this point. She just let herself bask in the unadulterated lust of two hot young men.

The kissing went on and on, sometimes two of them and sometimes all three. Rebecca was fascinated by watching the two boys kiss each other. The sound of their mouths melding together, and the smell of their hot sweet breath was making her ache, and she feared she would be up all night satisfying herself once she got home. She had no idea where this was going, but she was enjoying it.

Luke moved his arm from around Rebecca, kissed Ryan deeply, and rolled him onto his back. He sat up and straddled Ryan's hips, then lifted his skin-tight green shirt up and over his head. He threw it onto the pile where he had put Rebecca's bag, and she saw him in all his Adonis-like glory for the first time, and it took her breath away.

He had that perfect broad shouldered and narrow hipped shape that she loved, but she knew that already. Now she could see just how well sculptured his stomach and chest were, and Rebecca was sure she sighed out loud. He was gorgeous. Luke winked at her, and she knew she blushed at being caught staring.

Ryan lifted just the top half of his body like he was doing a sit up and removed his shirt too. Rebecca almost swooned. He was just as gorgeous as Luke. Same lovely broad shoulders and a seriously well-muscled chest with just the right amount of dark hair spreading nicely down his stomach to the waistband of his shorts, making Rebecca want to see more. Much more. Watching his abs ripple as he slowly lowered himself back onto the cushions made Rebecca moan out loud and both boys smiled.

Luke grinned and winked at Ryan who started to do the slowest, most sexually charged sit-ups Rebecca had ever seen. She knew for sure her knickers were getting wetter by the moment at the ostentatious display of masculine beauty.

Ryan reached out to Rebecca and pulled her to him. He kissed her, and she couldn't help running her hand over his chest and down his stomach. He lifted his hips and the feeling of his taut muscles under her fingertips was heavenly. Rebecca realised Luke was removing Ryan's shorts and tights, and she couldn't help letting her eyes wander down. But before she could see much of Ryan's cock, Luke had it in his mouth.

Far from disappointed, Rebecca watched in spellbound glory at the artistry of what Luke was doing to Ryan. They had very different styles, but both were as hot as hell to watch.

Ryan pulled Rebecca closer to him, held her head in his hands and kissed her passionately while Luke worked his magic on Ryan's cock. Rebecca was suddenly not sure this could possibly be real, but she intended to enjoy it as much as possible until the fantasy ended.

She couldn't taste Luke in Ryan's mouth anymore, but the sweet minty taste of his tongue lingered on her own as Luke took her hand to get her attention.

When she looked at Luke, he smiled and said, "Come help me here, Bec. Let's blow his mind."

She genuinely had no idea what Luke intended but she was keen to find out. She moved down to where Luke was kneeling over Ryan's cock and he moved a little to the side to make room for her.

"Suck him," Luke said. "Let me watch."

Rebecca was suddenly very self-conscious. She seemed to be in the presence of experts and wasn't sure she was that good. But she'd never had any complaints and this whole scenario was hotter than anything she had ever imagined, so she decided she was not letting any opportunity pass her by.

She took the head of Ryan's cock between her lips and began to massage it with her mouth and tongue until he was moaning quietly. Ryan put his hand down on her head and began running his fingers through her hair. Luke brushed the loose strands back off her face. "God that looks good, Bec,"

"Mmm. It feels good too," Ryan added and stroked her hair some more. Rebecca felt flattered that they both approved of what she was doing. As she continued, Luke moved to join her, licking and sucking Ryan's shaft then moving his mouth up to meet hers over the head of Ryan's cock. Luke and Rebecca kissed each other's lips and shared the rigid erection between them as if they were sharing a lollypop. Swapping it in and out of their warm wet mouths, taking turns to nibble, lick or suck. Constantly in motion over Ryan's throbbing member.

They began to move in sync, one either side of Ryan's cock, their lips and tongues meeting around the circumference as they repeatedly slipped and slid the full length of the delicious hard-on.

Ryan had a hand on each of their heads and was moaning and muttering and starting to squirm under their wanton ministrations. Rebecca felt Ryan tap her head gently and from Luke's reaction, she figured that meant Ryan was about to climax. Luke waited for just another beat or two before he took Ryan deep into his mouth and swallowed all of what Luke had to offer.

Rebecca squirmed as she watched Luke's lovely mouth and heard the exquisite sounds Ryan was making. As soon as Luke had sucked the last drops out of the now diminishing cock, Rebecca had to kiss him. She had to taste Ryan's come in Luke's mouth. She all but grabbed his face in her hands and pressed her tongue deep into his warm mouth. Luke returned her kiss eagerly and her yearning tongue was rewarded with the perfectly sweet and salty reminder of Ryan's pleasure.

Without taking his mouth off hers, Luke maneuvered Rebecca back onto the cushions beside Ryan, and he joined them in the pursuit of the last remaining taste of his own come in Luke's mouth.

Rebecca found herself lying in between two hot naked guys and almost couldn't believe it was real. Their kisses were sublime in their sensuality and Rebecca was lost in the tumbling sea of them.

As the heat of the kissing increased, Rebecca felt the boy's hands start to explore her body. She could feel they were touching her stomach and breasts, but the padding on her 'super smooth' bra was reducing the sensation. Although just the thought of it was enough to make her ache deeply between her legs.

Almost as if they were in sync with one another, the boys slipped the sequined braces off her shoulders and down past her waist. Luke cocked his head slightly and raised his eyebrows as if to check they could proceed. Rebecca nodded with a smile and tried not to look too desperate for their touch. Both boys smiled at her and Ryan slid his hand up her shirt and pushed the tight material up over her bra. She was suddenly very happy she had kept going to the gym instead of staying home to wallow in self-pity and chocolate after her break up with David.

"I think we can do without this spoilsport bra now," Luke said with a smirk as he undid the clasp at the front. "The shirt too I think."

They helped pull Rebecca's shirt up over her head and slide the bra straps off her arms. Her clothes were added to the growing pile and as soon as she laid back down Luke and Ryan each cupped one breast in their hands and began to kiss them. Their lips were warm but their kisses were hot, and as they each sucked a hard, aching nipple into their mouth Rebecca moaned loudly. She felt each boy smile.

For a time, she laid her head back, closed her eyes and let the sensations take her. She tried to make sense of the situation, but she couldn't. It was impossible to think with both her nipples being teased and sucked and licked at the same time. She opened her eyes and moved her head so that she could see the mouths that were giving her so much pleasure. The way the boys were sucking her and running their hands over her stomach and thighs was making her hotter and wetter than she had ever been, and she briefly wondered how she was ever going to come down.

Luke propped himself up on one elbow and began to just watch. He moved to touch Ryan's face and run his fingertips through his dark curls. "That looks so good baby," Luke said and cupped Ryan's cheek. Ryan turned his head briefly and kissed Luke's palm.

Watching that moment of tenderness, that loving exchange, made a light go on in Rebecca's lust-addled brain. She realised this was not some random hook up she had been drawn into. These boys were a couple, and a very loving couple by the looks of that.

She suddenly felt humbled and flattered to have been invited into this, to be asked to share this with these two beautiful boys.

"Show me, baby," Luke said softly. His hand still on Ryan's cheek.

Ryan opened his mouth to show Luke how his tongue was circling and teasing Rebecca's nipple. Then Luke moved his hand and joined in. Alternatively playing with the hard-sensitive nub or sliding his fingertip over Ryan's tongue and exploring his mouth.

Ryan closed his lips around Rebecca's nipple again, only this time Luke's finger was sharing the hot wetness and Rebecca moaned loudly.

Luke leant close to Rebecca and kissed her. Then he looked momentarily coy. "May I ask you a personal question, Bec?"

Rebecca was sure there were a hundred witty replies to that given the situation, but she couldn't think of any of them, so she simply replied, "Sure."

Luke smiled warmly but looked slightly uncomfortable. "We overheard you talking to Bryce earlier." He paused as if trying to form an idea into a sentence, but Ryan was doing such good things with his mouth while running his hand over her belly and thighs, and making her so hot, that she had almost forgotten they were in the middle of a conversation until Luke continued. "We were wondering, about your tests? Was everything okay?" he asked rather shyly, considering.

Rebecca was in such a whirl that her first thought was that this was an odd time to enquire about her health. But the look on Luke's face was almost pained and she suddenly realised what he was asking.

"Oh," she exclaimed. She wasn't sure how to answer at first. "Um...well yes, everything is fine."

Luke still didn't look satisfied. "Was it a special sort of check?" he asked suddenly looking very uncomfortable indeed.

Rebecca put her hand down on Ryan's head, drew him up to her mouth, and kissed him. She then kissed Luke and did her best to clear her head so that she could tell them what they wanted to know.

"My boyfriend, David, cheated on me. When I found out, we split up and I had a very thorough checkup with all the tests. They all came back clear and I've not been with anybody else since David." She took a deep breath and smiled at the boys. "Is that what you wanted to know?"

They both smiled very charming, boyish smiles and said, "Thank you."

Then, as if pre-choreographed, they worked to undo her hotpants and pull them and her tights off. Rebecca had a panicked moment of embarrassment when she realised she was wearing her very old, lucky Christmas undies. But everything came off and was in the pile so fast she figured nobody noticed. She was also momentarily embarrassed that she hadn't shaved her legs. Not that they were dreadful but still, David would have complained. But these two beautiful boys didn't seem to mind.

They laid her on her back, the three of them now naked, and began to run their fingertips and their lips all over her. It was magic and sent thrilling tingles bouncing up and down her spine. She closed her eyes and concentrated on the sound of their soft kisses and the feeling of every exquisite touch, like warm drops of rain on cool skin. She had not been touched since David and had never been touched the way they were touching her at all. Tears ran down the sides of her face and she hoped the boys didn't notice.

Soon enough though she had forgotten about tears as Luke began to kiss his way up her body to her mouth and Ryan began to kiss his way down to her feet.

"You are so beautiful, Bec," Luke said as he ran his hand down over her belly and gently cupped her mound. Rebecca gasped as he dipped his fingertips between her wet lips and easily found her clitoris and stroked it gently. "I want to go inside of you Rebecca," he whispered into her ear. "Is that okay?"

Rebecca couldn't speak, but she nodded. Luke smiled and kissed her deeply. As his tongue slid into her mouth, she felt him press his finger deep into her. She could feel Ryan's eyes on her, and when Luke whispered, "Spread your legs, beautiful, so Ryan can watch what I'm doing to you." It sent a wave of hot lust throughout her entire being.

She spread her legs and Luke pushed deep into her. She could feel her juices running down between her butt cheeks and she didn't think she had ever been that wet before. Luke moved to suck her nipple as he pushed two fingers into her and made her groan at the pressure inside her.

She could feel Ryan kissing his way up her inner thigh. She realised he was making his way to her aching hot pussy and she could barely breathe with the anticipation. When his lips finally touched hers, she gasped and felt Luke chuckle. He slid his fingers out of her pussy, and when she saw him slide them into Ryan's mouth, she felt her body tingle all over. Ryan licked and sucked Luke's fingers eagerly then moved back down to Rebecca's pussy and began to lick and suck there, with more enthusiasm than Rebecca had ever felt from a guy.

He ran his lips and tongue over every part of her, hungrily seeking out her most intimate, sensitive places. She felt Luke parting her lips and holding them to enable Ryan to press his tongue more deeply into her slippery wetness. "Spread more for us, beautiful, let us have all of you," he said in such a smooth sexy voice Rebecca almost melted.

She spread her legs as wide as she could and felt Ryan plunge deeply into her. Then Luke joined him and between the two of them, they were licking and lapping at her juices and teasing her clit and god knows what else. Rebecca didn't, all she knew was that two gorgeous hot guys were going down on her at the same time and she was lost in the slurping, slippery decadence of it all.

It wasn't long before Rebecca felt a deep warm glow building in her and she knew she was going to come. She couldn't speak but she needed them to know, she needed them to keep going and get her there. She reached down and rested her hands on their heads. One on Ryan's soft curls and one on Luke's silky blonde locks. She felt them both moan softly and she was sure they all understood each other.

She tried to relax. She had often struggled with reaching orgasm if she tried too hard. So, she did her best to trust that the boys knew what they were doing, and she was sure they did. Either one of them alone would have been the best she had ever had, so with both together, surely, they could get her some release. She tried to slow her mind, slow her breathing, and just let them have her. Let them take her and pleasure her and do as they wish with her. She could always get herself off at home if they didn't, she thought.

But she needn't have feared; in barely no time at all they had their tongues in sync around her clit and one or both had their fingers inside her massaging her g-spot. Rebecca exploded like the New Year's Eve fireworks over the harbour bridge as wave after sparkling wave of hot body slamming pleasure took complete possession of her entire being.

Initially, Rebecca had no awareness of her surroundings, but soon she realised that the boys had climbed up and were either side of her. All three of them were panting. She was glad of being sandwiched between their warm bodies. She felt a little chilled despite it being a hot summer night in Sydney, but they made her feel warm and comfortable.

Rebecca thought she may have slept a little, wrapped up in four strong arms. She wondered if the boys might have too, but she had no real idea. When she was next aware, she felt heavy as if she had just woken up, but she had never had a night like that one, so she couldn't tell.

"Hey, beautiful." Luke's warm voice sent a tingle up her spine. "How are you feeling?"

She rolled on her side to face him, and Ryan immediately moved to hug her back. She sighed at how good that felt.

She smiled at Luke and managed to say, "I'm feeling good."

"Pleased to hear it," he said, and Ryan kissed the back of her neck as if in agreement.

"Sorry to just spring that on you like that," Ryan spoke softly into her ear. "We had planned to ask you out, but I guess we got a bit ahead of ourselves."

Luke smiled and shrugged. "Can you forgive us?" he said.

Rebecca was still quite foggy and was not sure what was going on. She took a deep breath and tried to clear the cobwebs. "I'm sure there is nothing to forgive," she said. "That was the best night of my life."

Both boys seemed to relax, and they all fell silent for a little while until Rebecca asked, "You were going to ask me out? The two of you?"

"Yes," Luke said with a cheeky smirk. "Would you have said yes?"

"I guess we'll never know," Rebecca said, honestly not sure how she would have reacted. "Maybe, maybe not."

Ryan chuckled behind her. "Well, that's why we got cold feet," he confessed. "We were suddenly afraid you would say no."

Rebecca sat up to see if that helped her get her head around the conversation.

The boys sat up with her.

"Do you both ask girls out often?" she asked

Luke said, "We don't ask girls out often, hardly ever in fact. But we always ask them together. We are a package deal." He smiled and kissed her forehead.

"How long have you been a package deal?" Rebecca asked, trying to process everything and keep up despite still having a lot of brain fog in the way.

"Since high school," Ryan said behind her.

"We were best friends since infant's school," Luke said. "Then we both liked the same girl in high school and decided not to fight over her. She liked both of us, so she didn't mind if we shared, and we have been together ever since. Just not always with the same girl."

"And sometimes with no girl," added Ryan

"And currently no girl?" Rebecca asked

"Not since our last girlfriend went back home earlier this year," Luke said

"She was an international student," Ryan finished

Rebecca felt a bit like she was in the middle of a tennis game, but it was nice. Nice to hear two people so close and in tune with each other.

"So, will you?" Luke said, breaking Rebecca's train of thought.

"Will I what?" she asked perplexed.

"Will you go out with us?" both boys said at the same time.

"Define 'go out with,'" she said. She liked to know where she stood, and this was not something she was experienced in.

Both boys were quiet for a moment then Ryan said, "We'd like you to be our girlfriend. If you're comfortable with that."

Luke smiled at her and said, "Yes, just like a regular girlfriend only with two of us. Will you? Please, Rebecca? We'd be honoured if you would"

Rebecca laughed. This all felt so surreal but so comfortable and so...right, in an unexpected way.

"Why me?" she asked before she even knew she was going to.

They both laughed "You are hot for a start," Luke said.

"And kind."

"And smart. "

"And beautiful."

"And funny."

"And so comfortable with Bryce and that funny hand thing you do is so cute."

"And you don't care who sees it."

"And you totally rock those sequins, not every girl could do that."

It bounced back and forth until Rebecca was nearly dizzy. Eventually, she put up her hands to surrender. "Okay, okay already, I'll go out with you. Now stop before you flatter me to death."

Luke smiled a radiant, beaming smile and she could sense that Ryan was doing the same.

Then, all of a sudden, she was engulfed in a sea of hands and arms and mouths as both boys began to kiss her all over. She laughed at their puppy-like playfulness and felt very lucky. Then it dawned on her that she had two boyfriends and she started to giggle.

The three of them descended into a giggling, laughing mess with much tickling and by the time Rebecca had settled down she was on her back and had a mouth on each nipple and two hands between her thighs teasing and playing with her soft lips.

"Careful. You'll get me all wet again," she said.

Luke looked up and winked at her. "You've spotted our cunning plan," he said.

Rebecca laughed then laid back and let her boys play. It felt so natural, she struggled to imagine how she had never considered such a thing before.

Soon she struggled to imagine anything at all as the boys were diligently working to get her as hot and wet as they could, very successfully too. She found herself with Luke's warm wet mouth on hers while he played with her nipples and breasts with one dexterous hand. She writhed under his touch while Ryan's mouth worked hot magic on her pussy.

She was so turned on she thought she might implode.

Luke whispered in her ear, "We want you, sweet thing. We want to have you completely. Are you okay with that?"

She smiled, knowing she would let them. She wanted them just as much, but she was feeling playful as well as horny. She turned her head and smiled at Luke. "So, you want me to put out, on a first date, with two guys?" she teased and kissed his nose.

"Well technically, given that we are still at work, this isn't a date at all. So basically, we want you to put out *before* the first date... and yes with two guys."

"Well," she said with a barely suppressed giggle. "I'm not sure how my boyfriends will feel about that."

Ryan stopped what he was doing and looked up along Rebecca's naked body and said, "They approve wholeheartedly."

"Yep, they do," Luke said.

"Well then," Rebecca said. "I reckon it must be okay if both my boys agree."

Luke kissed her deeply and Ryan moved his tongue to her clit, and within moments she was moaning a deep warm orgasm into Luke's mouth.

Ryan moved up and Luke greedily kissed the wetness off his face before they laid either side of Rebecca and held her while she basked in the afterglow.

"Honey," Luke said in her ear. "We have condoms in Ryan's bag. We'd rather not use them. But we are fine if you aren't comfortable with that yet. We are clean though, we would never endanger you or each other."

Rebecca thought about that for just a moment. She felt safe, and she trusted them, but she still said, "Do you really have condoms?"

"Sure," Ryan said and reached for his bag. "We are happy to use them if it makes you more comfortable, beautiful. That's why we bought them."

"We don't even have to go that far at all sweetness," Luke added. "You're just so hot we got a bit carried away, but we can stop here and take things more slowly."

"Yes, sorry, Bec honey. We didn't mean to be pushy. We can go as slow as you like," Ryan added

They both kissed her and held her. No pressure, no badgering, even though she knew they were horny as hell. She felt tears welling in her eyes, but she was determined not to cry. She felt like she was lost in a beautiful, impossible dream.

"I want you," she whispered quietly. "Please, I want you to make love to me. Both of you, the way you want to."

She felt Ryan move as if reaching for his bag again. "No, you don't need that," she said.

"You sure?" they asked in unison.

"Perfectly sure," she said. "Take me now, please."

Both boys kissed her deeply, passionately and thoroughly, leaving her close to panting, then Luke said, "Close your eyes, Princess, and let your boys have their way with you."

Rebecca closed her eyes and the boys stretched her out on the cushions. She felt their mouths all over her and their fingers between her lips, playing, teasing, turning her on even more. Then wordlessly she felt a hand grab each ankle and lift her legs up high and wide apart. She felt one hot body move between her thighs, she had no idea who. Then fingers spread her lips apart, and she felt the slippery head of a hard cock pressed against her. She could feel one of her boys was guiding the other one inside of her, but she had no idea who was doing what. The pleasure that knowledge gave her was indescribable and flooded her with a tingling warmth.

She closed her eyes tighter and tilted her head to the ceiling. She didn't want to accidentally see which one was which. She felt the pressure gradually increasing. She could feel herself being slowly, exquisitely, stretched around the rigid head and knew it must look so good.

Finally, she had the head inside of her, and she felt one of her boys straddle her waist and the grip on her ankles changed, and she felt hands on her thighs as well. Then with one slow hard push, she had the entire rigid cock deep inside her.

The sensation was indescribable. He just held himself there, still and hard, deep in her for a delicious eternity. Then he slowly slid out a little and pressed deep again. Each time he pressed into her, Rebecca felt almost faint from pleasure. It was like he was using his rock-hard cock to massage her from the inside. She felt so full and so wet and so turned on she never wanted it to stop, but after only a little while she felt the gorgeous hardness pull right out of her, and she sighed.

The grip on her ankles changed again, and whichever hot guy was straddling her moved and was replaced. She realised they were changing places.

Again, she felt the hands of one of her boys guiding the head of the other's hard-on between her eager wet lips. Again, she felt the glorious slow stretch and push and the changing of the grip. She imagined in her head how it must look. One hot naked guy straddling her waist, holding her ankles and spreading her legs wide apart while the other one pressed his cock deep into her, over and over again.

She kept her eyes closed and was suddenly flushed with the idea that she had been fucked by two different guys within moments of each other. The blushing warmth of her cheeks gradually spread out and caused a rush of new wetness around the cock inside of her. Both boys moaned so they must have felt or seen it and that made Rebecca even hotter. After nowhere near enough, Rebecca felt her boy pull out of her, and she groaned in protest.

Both boys then moved from where they were to either side of her, and she felt them both whisper, "Thank you," and kiss her face.

"Open your eyes now, beautiful," Luke said

"And roll over for me Princess," Ryan requested.

Rebecca opened her eyes and rolled over, blinking as she adjusted to the light. Ryan moved behind her, put a hand on each hip and said, "Come back on me beautiful, I want to fuck you properly now."

Rebecca moved up on to her hands and knees and Luke helped guide her back onto Ryan's cock. He guided Ryan into her again and said, "God that looks good," as Ryan began to fuck Rebecca. He moved slowly at first but as she started to move back and meet each thrust, he pushed harder and faster.

Rebecca loved it from behind like that. It was one of the positions that gave her the freedom to tilt her hips so that she was being touched in just the right places inside.

She looked back over her shoulder to see Luke mesmerised by the movement of Ryan's cock in and out of her. That gave her a deep thrill, but she was hungry for something extra.   "Please, Luke, I want you in my mouth."

He grinned broadly and moved himself in front of Rebecca to present his cock for her enjoyment. She ran her tongue over the top of it and took just the head into her mouth. It was hard and slippery and tasted of her own juices, and that made her ache. Luke held her head gently in his hands and let her explore him with her mouth.

His cock was almost identical to Ryan's in its shape and size, but as she enjoyed him in her mouth, she realised he tasted a little different. She decided she needed to explore that more, so she licked and sucked and teased every sensitive area she could find to make him start to ooze his flavour into her mouth, so she could learn him and know him and be able to tell who she had in her mouth.

As the intensity of Ryan's fucking grew, so did her hunger for Luke's cock. She slid as much of him into her mouth as she could manage, tightened her lips around him and let the pounding of Ryan's cock move her up and down Luke's shaft, while her tongue danced around the sensitive head each time he was drawn out far enough.

She could hear both her boys moaning and muttering, and that made her happy. She began to push herself back hard onto every thrust of Ryan's cock and could feel he was on the verge of coming. She slammed back on every thrust and felt him grip her hips tightly as he made the most exquisite groaning noise, and she could feel his cock twitching and pulsating inside her.

Luke held her face gently, brushed the hair out of her eyes, and said, "Hey precious, I'm happy to come in your mouth if that's what you want, but I'd really like something else."

Rebecca smiled, even with a mouth full of Luke's cock. She couldn't deny that she wanted to have him in her mouth, but she also wanted him everywhere else. So, she slowly let him slide out from between her lips and smiled at him. "What did you have in mind?" she said.

Luke laid down on his back "Come fuck me, precious."

Rebecca didn't need to be asked twice. She straddled him and engulfed his cock almost in one smooth move. Luke groaned. Rebecca put her hands on his chest and began to slowly ride him, moving and tilting her hips to find the way he felt best inside her. Ryan knelt behind her and sat her up, so he could put his arms around her. He cupped her breasts and kissed her neck and shoulders.

"You're so beautiful," he whispered softly in her ear. "So fucking beautiful. Hold still and let Luke do the work, Princess. I want to feel your body while he fucks you."

Rebecca held still over Luke and let him fuck her at his own speed. She rested her head on Ryan's shoulder and closed her eyes and concentrated on all the sensations. Luke's cock inside of her, Ryan's hands moving over her stomach and breasts, his warm, soft lips and the slight graze of stubble on her neck and shoulders.

She could feel his perfect hard body against her back, and it added to her heat. She wanted to be sandwiched between both of them, pressed tight. She wanted to feel their weight on her. But that could wait, she thought, and the sudden realisation that she would be making love to these two hot guys as much as she wanted, overwhelmed her and she had to press back harder on Ryan's strong chest to ground herself.

He put his arm around her waist to steady her. He ran a hand down her belly and rested it on her mound the way Luke had before, dipping the tips of his fingers between her puffy wet lips to find her blood-filled nub. She moaned. She could smell the sweet warmth of his breath as he whispered gently in her ear, "I want you to come for me, Princess. Can you do that? Come for me while our boy fucks you."

Rebecca tried to answer, but she was breathless. She found it hard to do anything but moan, as Ryan began to work her clit and Luke fucked her like they both knew exactly what they were doing. She could feel the heat building under Ryan's fingertips and the deep pleasure inside her, moving and growing, becoming connected, and she knew she was going to come.

"Look at our boy," Ryan encouraged. "Look at that body, all those muscles working just to fuck you, precious. Beautiful, isn't he? And all ours, just ours. Now play with your nipples, Princess, and let him see how lucky he is."

Rebecca put her hands on her breasts and started to play with her nipples. She had never really done that very much but as soon as she did Luke moaned and began to fuck her harder. She pressed back into Ryan's arms, and he worked on her clit, and the sensations all blended together until her head was a whirl. She felt like an overfilled balloon ready to burst. She was so grateful for Ryan's arm around her waist or she feared she would collapse.

"That's my good girl," Ryan purred. "Come for us, let him feel it, good girl."

As Ryan's breath cascaded across her skin, her knees began to tremble and every sensation in her body crashed together. She cried out as the pleasure almost knocked her over. Ryan held her tight as the walls of her pussy spasmed around Luke's cock and she heard him cry out just moments after her. She could feel him coming inside her, and she wanted to smile at the thought, but she was lost so deep in a happy glow that she wasn't sure if her face was still connected to her thoughts.

Ryan kissed her neck, made some warm, soothing sounds that may or may not have been words and gently let her down into Luke's waiting arms. Luke held her as she nestled into his chest and, aside from noticing he was still inside her, she wasn't sure she had any grasp on reality any more.

When she was next aware of her surroundings she was on her side in Luke's arms with Ryan at her back. She could feel Ryan had a hard-on and she pressed herself back on it and moaned.

"Careful, Princess." Luke smiled at her and brushed the hair off her face and kissed her forehead. "You'll get him started again."

"Mmm," she said sleepily as she pressed her backside against Ryan's cock again. "You've spotted my cunning plan."

"Does our girl want more?" Luke asked with a grin

"I reckon she does," Rebecca said and pressed Ryan again. This time he had hold of his cock and moved the head between her thighs.

"Tilt for me Princess, and I'll give you what you need," Ryan said from behind.

Rebecca tilted her hips back, and Luke put his hand down between her legs to guide Ryan's cock into her. She was such a wet mess down there he slipped in easily and she gasped. She was a little sore, but the slight sting felt good.

"You okay, baby?" Luke asked.

"Yes," she said as Ryan began to move slowly inside her. "Just a little sore but it feels deeply good."

Luke raised his eyebrows and grinned. "I can always kiss it better baby."

"Mmm," was about all Rebecca could manage as Ryan's cock was rubbing on her g-spot just perfectly.

Luke seemed to vanish and reappear facing the other way. Without hesitation he was face down between her thighs. Ryan spread her legs by pulling one up and over his thighs, giving Luke better access, and she felt his tongue press deep between her lips, licking Ryan's cock as it slid in and out of her. She almost spun out at the thought at that but was instead distracted by the notion that Luke's cock was very close to her mouth. She put a hand on his backside to signal what she wanted, and soon enough the three of them wiggled into a position, lying on their sides, where Rebecca could basically sixty-nine with Luke while Ryan fucked her from behind.

She was in some decadent heaven and never wanted to leave it.

In moments Luke was hard in her mouth, and she tried to focus on giving him the best head she could under the circumstances.

They got into a perfect rhythm, Luke shared his attentive and magic tongue between her clit and Ryan's cock, she sucked Luke's cock like it was going to save her life, and Ryan fucked her hard and strong as he held her tight while whispering sweet dirty words in her ear.

Rebecca had no idea how long it went on for, but at some point, the energy in the room moved up a few degrees and Luke was suddenly sucking her clit hard into his mouth and lashing it with his tongue as Ryan pounded her and talked so dirty, she almost blushed.

She could feel they were all building to a climax that seemed beyond anything any of them could control. If not for the cock in her mouth, she was sure she would be screaming like a banshee as the pleasure built up to a point beyond anything she had ever imagined.

The hot salty sweat of their bodies made them slip and slide all over each other and sounds of lust filled the air like pealing bells. She felt stubble, she felt lips and tongues. She felt hands and cocks and steaming, hot, muscled bodies writhing either side of her, sandwiching her, compressing her, just the way she wanted. She could feel the corrugations of heaving abs pressed against her and the straining muscles of backs and thighs. The three of them seemed lost in the pursuit of unadulterated pleasure.

Her heart was bellowing in her ears, and she could barely catch her breath as Luke thrust his cock into her mouth over and over and held her clit between his teeth, frantically moving his merciless tongue like he was trying to erase it. The three of them were trembling, almost uncontrollably, and Ryan was grunting and moaning behind her and filling her eager hungry pussy over and over and over with his pounding hard cock until...

The three of them fell silent almost simultaneously, totally silent as if they were in suspended animation. Then barely a heartbeat later, one by one they screamed and groaned and all but howled as they exploded in near unison. Ryan first, spurting and twitching his burning come into her equally hot depths. Then Luke, spilling himself eagerly in spasms into her willing, wanton mouth. Rebecca swallowed as much as she could before she was hit by the mother of all orgasms, squealing and whimpering as it washed over her like a tsunami of molten pleasure. She came with more intensity than she ever would have believed possible. She might have examined that further but the capacity for speculative thought had left her. In fact, the capacity for any thought at all had left her, and she simply existed in an afterglow so radiant she had to close her eyes.

When Rebecca opened her eyes, she felt mildly irritated but couldn't fathom why. It took her a moment to realise the irritation was being caused by her alarm buzzing on her bedside table. She felt heavy and confused and not entirely sure she hadn't been out on the drink the night before. She lay there for a while wondering how the heck she got home... and from where. She rolled over and the smarting sting between her legs brought the night before flooding back in vivid detail, and she smiled involuntarily.

For a brief moment, she wondered if it had been a dream, but there was no way a dream was going to make her that sore. She calculated she must have had about two months' worth of sex in a couple of hours.

Boy was it going to sting to pee, she thought, and laughed out loud. She replayed things in her head and revelled in how it made her feel. Most of the night was clear and vivid but getting home was still patchy. She remembered being bundled up snug in the passenger seat while Luke drove her car...but where was Ryan? Then she remembered the motorbike pulling up next to them at the lights and Luke leaning out to kiss the leather-clad rider.

She could recall how good the shower felt. Thank God for removable shower heads she thought, but the rest of it was a blur. Maybe it would come back. She sunk back into her pillow and was dozing off when her phone pinged. She was too close to sleep to be able to react until it pinged again. She couldn't fathom who would be messaging her so insistently first thing in the morning, but with the third ping, her brain clicked on and she pounced on the phone to see three messages from 'her boys' and everything moved from potential dream to beautifully real.

'Good morning beautiful xxx'

'We miss you already xxx'

'And Merry Christmas'

The third message sent a wave of panic through Rebecca. How did she forget it was Christmas? What the hell time was it? Holy fuck she couldn't remember locking up the shop.

The phone pinged again

'Relax, Princess, we locked up and set the alarm. All is well.'

Rebecca almost looked around for a camera then smiled at her silliness.

'And no, you didn't leave your lucky Christmas undies in the kiddies castle. We confiscated them, so you wouldn't be getting lucky with anybody else this Christmas. '

Rebecca laughed and replied.

'Are you kidding? I have no intention of getting lucky with anybody else for the rest of my life!'

The barrage of happy emojis that followed with a message about Santa bringing them just what they wanted, made her laugh harder than she had in a long time.

She dragged herself out of bed and headed for the shower, stepping over her discarded clothes from the night before and grinning widely. She headed out the door with moments to spare to get to her grandparent's on time. She and Bryce would be forgiven for not helping with the preparations, but they would help with the dishes as they usually did.

When she got there, everybody was busy doing something in the kitchen or out at the barbeque where the tables were set up.

Grandad was entertaining the smaller kids, as always, and Bryce was late, as always. It was a perfectly normal Christmas except she kept getting messages from her two gorgeous lovers, which left her grinning like a fool and trying to hide her happiness. At least for now. At least until it was more real, and she could think about it without blushing. Then she wondered when she was going to get a chance to tell Bryce, given that he didn't show up until they were about to sit down and eat.

He looked like the cat that caught the canary all through lunch and she wondered what he'd been up to, but figured she would find out when they were alone, and would trump whatever it was with her evening's adventures. Rebecca's pocket was buzzing every few minutes. The dinner table was meant to be a phone free zone, but she did keep peeking whenever she could. Her boys were promising to shave her legs for her in a long soaking bubble bath followed by a slow all over massage and a night of gentle love making if she felt up to it. She was sure she would, one way or another.

When lunch was finally over, and all the gifts were exchanged, Bryce and Rebecca headed to the kitchen for scullery duty. When they were alone, Bryce threw his arms around Rebecca and said, "I found the perfect gift for you gorgeous."

She interrupted, wanting to tell him about her night but he shushed her. "Age before beauty, pumpkin," he said and held up a USB stick.

She was busting to tell him but figured she would let him have his fun first. She reached to take the USB stick, a little perplexed but more focussed on her news than the gift, if she was totally honest.

Bryce pulled it back and didn't let her have it. Then he grinned the most evil grin she had ever seen and said, "Did none of you read the sign above the door on your way in?"

"What sign?" Rebecca asked

"The one that clearly says 'Your children may be video recorded while in this castle.' There are three cameras in there, honey. Did none of you think to look?"

Rebecca went pale. The security cameras! She never thought of that. Holy fuck, she thought, if Grandpa sees that he will have another stroke…and it beamed straight back to the security firm. She could just see it ending up on youtube.

Bryce grabbed her and sat her on a chair before she fainted.

"Relax. honey, I didn't mean to scare you. It's all fine. It isn't part of the main system, it is only connected to my computer, so it's only me baby girl, only me. You're safe."

He handed her a glass of water, and she sipped it slowly.

She looked up into his eyes a little coyly and then they both grinned. "I guess that saves me having to tell you my news then?" she said still feeling a little weak.

"Sure does, honey. In fact, I could tell you a thing or two I reckon. I didn't have my eyes shut half the time!"

"You watched it!" She slapped his upper arm "Perve," she teased with a laugh.

"In my defence," he said. "I got a notification that the cameras were activated, and I was watching the boys, obviously, and by the time you came in I was hooked. Besides I needed to make sure you were okay." He winked. "So, I had front row seats to the live streaming, honey, but of course I didn't look." He put his hand over his eyes but with his fingers spread like a small child peeking at hide and seek.

"And this," he said handing her the USB finally. "is all of the recordings from the three cameras. The only copies in existence, encrypted and protected by our secret password for you to keep safe. If you're ever tempted to watch it back, I suggest you only watch the file I've labelled 'The Perfect Gift.' It has been beautifully edited, if I do say so myself, and I cut out the bit where you didn't want to see who went first. That looked like a bit of a sacred ritual, and I thought you might prefer not to know. And they are right you know, you do totally rock those sequins. I said you would!"

"There's audio?" she exclaimed.

"Oh yes, honey, not a sight or sound missed," he smirked. "And very clear too considering the low light. I think they are the luckiest boys alive, Bec honey, and you deserve every perfect bit of them. But if they hurt you, I will strap them down and cut off their balls."

"You never threatened to cut off David's balls," she said amused.

"Eew," Bryce said and screwed up his face as if he'd been poisoned. "I don't even want to think about his balls, thank you very much. I don't know what you ever saw in him."

Rebecca stood up and hugged her cousin and tears streamed down her cheeks as her pocket pinged with the sort of attention she never really knew how much she had ached for, until now. "Me neither," she all but sobbed. "Thank you. cuz. It is the perfect gift, and I am the luckiest girl alive. Merry Christmas."

*****

The Night Before Christmas

'T was the night before Christmas when all through the house, not a creature was stirring, not even a...

Well, she thought, she had no idea what the mice may or may not be up to. But here in the upstairs bedroom of a quaint old house, there was plenty going on. She looked around and noted her subjects, nicely bound and looking terrified, and she smiled. Just the way she liked them.

She had driven to the agreed address in a very chirpy mood, listening to Bing Crosby on the radio and feeling good. She didn't often work Christmas Eve, but this was an extremely well-paying gig and she had no other plans, so she jumped at the chance. She had been doing this sort of work for a long time, so she enjoyed a bit of variety. Who wouldn't? Taking this gig rather than passing it on to one of her staff was her Christmas gift to herself.

She had been planning the scene all week, making sure she packed all of what might be needed into her very large, purpose-built bag. It was black sturdy leather with good solid handles and was affectionately known as the mobile dungeon. She always had it stocked with the basics but would top it up with more specialty items as the need arose.

This gig certainly required some specialty items. The brief initially had her entering the house via the chimney but she did have to draw the line somewhere, so instead she had packed her small lock pick set. Technically it was illegal for her to have these tools, but just sitting in her bag, the set looked like an innocent manicure set. If she had any trouble she knew a locksmith who would happily say he accidentally left them in her car. In the worst case, she knew a whole bunch of policemen, lawyers, and judges who would help her out.

She looked over at her subjects again and thought they had been a little too easy to subdue, taking the edge off it for her a little. But this was not about her needs; this was about giving the client the very best erotic fantasy experience money could buy and so to that end she had planned a perfect evening for them. If she enjoyed it too, that was a bonus.

She had found the place and managed to break in with no trouble at all. The layout of the house was exactly as she had been told, so finding the master bedroom had been simple and she managed to subdue the couple easily. So far, things were going to plan.

She loved the meticulous planning, sometimes more than the execution. Taking what the client wanted or needed as part of their fantasy and weaving it into a narrative that pleased her and would satisfy them made her happy. Adding her own special touches to make it her scene, her art, without detracting from the client's needs...that was the pearl in the oyster.

She unpacked her bag and placed everything in her preferred order, just where she wanted it. She liked order. Her various toys and implements were spread on an intricately carved box at the end of the ornate four-poster bed. She loved rich old kinksters. The floggers and paddles were easily within arm's reach, and the stockings were hung around the bedpost with care in the knowledge that they would be in use very soon.

She looked over at the client and smiled to herself at how helpless he looked and how handy the small leather bit gag was to subdue unnecessary conversation. She would normally have used duct tape, but the client's full white beard made that impossible. Luckily she always had a Plan B. They'd done enough talking already, albeit primarily via email. But there had been plenty of communication back and forth about how things would work. Not just about the client's needs but about what she needed to make sure the whole scene was safe and hopefully enjoyable.

Making sure there were no kids in the house and establishing the boundaries, limits, and safe words or signals with the client - or in this case, clients - were kind of the boring but necessary parts of the job for her. She shouldn't have to tell people not to have the kids in the next room while they are having their flesh expertly flogged by a woman in leather and stilettos, but she felt compelled to remind people of that. These clients, however, already had that under control.

The children had been packed off for the holidays so presumably they were somewhere safe, nestled snug in their beds while, no doubt, visions of sugar plums danced in their heads. She grinned at that thought and also at the thought that she was here, about to do all manner of naughty things to their parents. Or were they the grandparents? It was hard to tell; they didn't look young.

She walked in a slow circle around the man she had bound hand and foot to the chair beside the bed. His red flannel pyjama pants around his ankles added to the demeaning nature of his predicament. She traced the tip of her favourite red and black leather riding crop across his jaw and watched the pulse in his neck pound. She brought the crop down in one stinging blow across his inner thigh and watched the tears run silently down his cheeks.

"That's my good boy," she said, tapping the shaft of the crop menacingly across her palm. She loved the way the whites of his eyes grew large and his pupils dilated. No matter how many times she saw that fear response in a client, it still gave her an almost guilty thrill.

She grabbed the white fir trim at the front of his red flannel top and tore the garment open, exposing a fat belly, covered in white hair. He must be older than I think, she thought.

He gasped as the buttons flew in all directions. She brought the crop down on his thigh again in exactly the same spot and relished his almost silent flinching, "I did tell you what would happen if you made a sound," she said calmly, squeezing his cheeks beneath his snow-white beard between her thumb and fingers. "And now I have to gag you better to keep you quiet."

She picked up one stocking from the bedpost and ran it through her fingers slowly, sensually as he watched. Beads of sweat appeared on his forehead and chest. She moved the gag for the moment to force his mouth open and then fed the stocking slowly into it. She was in no rush. They had all night and she knew that the anticipation was often more delicious than the release. She fed the entire stocking into his mouth, almost painfully slowly, and then picked up the second one, twining it delicately between her fingers before gradually stuffing it in with its pair.

She removed the black bit gag from where it had slipped to around his neck and took a different, small red leather gag from the bed. She placed it over the stocking stuffed mouth of the fat old man and fastened it tight. Then she circled him again and found pleasure in his sweat-soaked forehead. But the night was young, and she didn't want it cut short by anything avoidable, like a health crisis, so she went to the window and threw up the sash.

She had wondered about their choice of nightwear for a hot summer night in Sydney, but if it was part of their fantasy, she would work with it. When she had 'broken in,' they looked as if they were dressed for the north pole and had just settled down for a long winter's nap. So, she did need to be mindful of overheating.

There was a light cooling breeze outside. She stood by the open window and gazed out for a while. The moon was full and gave a lustre of mid-day to objects on the lawn below. She saw scattered bikes and toys, including a miniature sleigh and eight tiny reindeer.

She moved back into the room and noticed he had cooled off a bit. She moved to him, grabbed the edge of his white y-front underpants, and tore them open in one carefully practised move to expose a small flacid penis that she immediately laughed at, knowing he would like that. "No wonder your wife has to look elsewhere for a decent fuck," she said. He made a muffled sound, but she ignored it. She went to the end of the bed and found a small metal cage. "And lucky I brought the extra small cage with me," she laughed

She approached him and grabbed his penis with deft, practised hands so that in barely a moment she had encased his dick in the small cage. "That will keep your sad little cock out of the way while I have some fun with your hot slut of a wife," she said. The look on his face was worth every second of the week's preparations. She felt her pulse quicken and noticed her body responding in ways it didn't often do anymore.

He made a muffled groaning sound again and she slapped his face with the unexpected speed and severity of an eagle snaring its prey. His cheek was suddenly almost as red as his flannel nightcap. Another odd choice for summer she thought. She shouted at him and called him by name. "Now, Nicholas, I've warned you if there is another sound you will be severely punished." She knew he would make another sound, she would make sure of that. But it was time to move things along a bit.

She checked that his bonds were well fastened and, once happy with her work, she turned her attention to the woman lying on the bed. The woman had her wrists bound to a metal bar with broad black leather cuffs. The bar was then chained to the edge of the bed, holding the woman's arms above her head.

The helpless woman's ankles were fastened to a similar bar that held her legs wide apart, having the effect of pushing her night dress up past her hips. This was made worse when the 'intruder" pulled the rope she had attached to a pully on the beam of the bed canopy and pulled the woman's legs high into the air so that her hips were barely touching the mattress.

"Now Mary, did your mother never tell you not to show your underwear to strangers?"

The look of fear, shame, and humiliation on the bound woman's face was so exquisite that her tormentor had to turn her head for a moment to compose herself. She hadn't had to do that for years, but she was very much enjoying her work tonight. She was beginning to feel quite aroused and she liked that, but it did require more discipline on her part. Not a bad thing to be reminded of from time to time.

She ran the tip of her crop down Mary's naked leg and felt her victim quake with fear. It was moments like those that made the job worthwhile. She felt her body respond and grinned to herself at the realisation of just how much she was enjoying this.

"Nice legs, Mary. I bet you were a dancer. I can just see you prancing on those nice pins. Teasing and flirting with all the boys and never giving them the chance to follow through. Yet here you are on your back with those pretty legs in the air just showing your underwear to all, and offering yourself up to me like a bitch in heat. My dirty little vixen." She ran the tip of the crop up and down the quaking woman's thighs and over the damp gusset of her very sensible underwear.

"You are such a dirty girl aren't you Mary?" she said, giving the damp patch just a small slap with the crop. Just a delicious teasing tap or two. Well, more like three or four before she realised it was sending an enormous thrill through her own body and making her wet. She decided it was time to move on, but not until she had made just a couple more strikes and then rubbed the tip quite firmly over the whole, now wet, crotch.

She stepped away for a moment to regain her composure. This was turning into a fun gig and it was only going to get better from here. She put down her crop and moved onto the bed, beside the trembling body of the helpless woman, showing her a small sharp knife with an ornately carved bone handle. The woman's eyes were wide with terror, but she said nothing. The ball gag in her mouth may have had something to do with that. She did cast her eyes over her client's hands just to be sure no sign of true distress was apparent before she began to slowly slice the night dress. She cut the fabric into long strips and then cut the strips into small pieces but left it largely in place until she was done.

Then with almost frantic movements, she dashed the fragments of fabric away and they flew everywhere like dry leaves in a wild hurricane. When all the fabric was gone, she looked at the newly exposed breasts. Large, well worn, soft breasts with enormous dark nipples surrounded by very large close to black areolas almost too big to fit in her palm.

She pinched the nipples until they were hard, and Mary groaned. "If you make too much noise Mary, I will have to punish you." She pinched the nipples hard and twisted them until Mary whimpered around the gag. She was enjoying the sounds that Mary was making and the look on Mary's face so much that she felt her own nipples begin to throb and a nice warm feeling spread from between her legs up to her navel.

She grabbed handfuls of Mary's breasts and squeezed them then trailed her fingers down her mature matronly body to the edge of her underwear. The white cotton fabric was no obstacle and she cut the last vestiges of Mary's modesty off as she had done with the nightgown, exposing a mass of dark curly hair. She grabbed a handful of the full bush, something she didn't often get to do, and pulled hard. Mary tried to squeal, but it was no more than a muffled cry.

She pulled again and revelled in the sounds Mary made. "You know I'm going to have to punish you now Mary, don't you?" she said as she got off the bed and pulled the rope to lift Mary's legs higher. She grabbed Mary's bush with two hands and pulled apart her soft ripe lips and found what she was looking for. "You are very wet, Mary. See, I knew you were a dirty slut and I'm going to fuck you like one. But just before I do, I always like to make a mark to remember me by." She grabbed her knife and with lightning speed made a tiny nick on Mary's thigh. As a drop of red blood oozed out slowly, she dipped her finger in it, grabbed her crop, and walked over to Nicholas.

Each step she took reminded her of just how aroused she was becoming and just how wet she was getting. She thought some of her own toys would be getting quite a workout tonight when she got home and could replay this scene over in her head to have some real fun.

She stood in front of Nicholas and slowly licked the bright red drop off her finger before she said, "Look at that, Nicholas, your wife's fresh red blood. I could do anything to her and you have let yourself be made powerless to stop me. You pathetic little man. Can't protect your wife. Can't even fuck her like she needs it. Lucky for her, I am about to fuck her in ways she has never imagined, and you can't do anything but watch. You can't even get a hard-on over it," she said, flicking the tiny caged cock with the end of her crop and revelling in his terrified expression.

She moved back over to Mary slowly, enjoying every second of the anticipation in the air and every thrilling sensation between her own legs. She picked up a bag full of toys and gently flung a bundle of them on the bed. She was going to enjoy this, she could tell already, as there was a slight tremor in her knees while she looked into the collection.

She pulled out an assortment and showed them to Mary. "Look, Mary, you are about to get the fucking you have been craving followed by the punishment a filthy whore like you deserves." She held up each item until she found one that got a good reaction out of Mary. Once she had selected the tool, she pressed the head of the large glass dildo against Mary's wet lips and pushed it hard into her. Despite the gag, the noises Mary made were clear and distinctive, and her tormentor loved them. She plunged the dildo in and out of Mary until she could feel the woman was clearly building to orgasm.

"See, Nicholas, a piece of glass is a better fuck than you. Listen to the noise your filthy slut of a wife is making when I jam it into her." She continued until she was sure Mary had climaxed. She was going to slide it out and change tack, but she changed her mind. She was enjoying herself so much she continued until she was sure Mary was on the brink of a second orgasm. Then she expertly held Mary there, on the edge of the abyss, teetering between release and crushing disappointment, for a truly evil eternity.

Mary was whimpering and quivering, tears streaming down her cheeks until her captor let her have her climax and the sound of it was its own reward. She struggled to not orgasm herself at the unadulterated power trip that Mary's predicament was giving her. She finally slid the dildo out of the sopping wet pussy. She glanced over at Nicholas and saw that he was spellbound by what she was doing to his wife and that his cock had swollen to the maximum it could in its cage, straining against its bonds. Good, she thought.

She reached into the toy selection and brought out a vibrator with a little rabbit attachment. Mary groaned, as it was shoved right up inside her and switched on. The attachment was pressed hard against Mary's clitoris. It looked like a small woodland creature that danced around on the head of Mary's clit like a tiny deer pummelling her bead of pleasure and prancing and pawing at her lust with its tiny hoof.

She pressed it deep into Mary who was squirming and sweating and struggling against her bonds as did many women who love to be bound. They loved to struggle against the strength, the power. She understood that; she loved to be that strength and power and be fruitlessly struggled against. It made her hot and caused her to ache deep between her legs.

She looked across at Nicholas, red-cheeked and with a nose like a cherry, his clothes in disarray and practically shredded and hanging off him, with pieces of Mary's night dress in tatters around him. She could see his jaw clenching as if biting the stockings between his teeth. The fluffy white hair poking out from under his cap was almost like a wreath around his head. She looked carefully and decided that in spite of his dishevelled appearance, there was a twinkle in his eye. He was enjoying this. They all were, she thought, and grinned to herself. She knew she was, as unprofessional as that might be.

She brought her mind back to her work. Mary was on the verge of coming again and she encouraged it. But Mary was squirming away from the direct stimulation of her clit. She was determined to give this client more pleasure than anybody had bargained for. So, she kept the vibrations focused on Mary's sensitive nub despite her thrashing about and they were all soon rewarded with the best muffled screams of pleasure anybody could imagine.

She had to focus hard to not be reckless in her work but was wet, soaking wet, and so aroused it was difficult. She slid the toy out of Mary and stepped away for a moment or two to regain her focus. It would not do to get too far off course with such high paying clients. She was in control and she had to maintain that. She hadn't had to give herself that talk for over a decade; it actually pleased her that she could still get so turned on. But she still had work to do.

She strapped her most powerful vibrator to Mary's thigh with the head positioned directly on the unwilling clit. She got a large ribbed dildo and slid it up inside the wet hairy pussy and turned on the vibrator. Almost immediately Mary was making the most exquisite sounds, albeit a little muffled, and she could see the wetness pouring out of Mary's pussy. She smiled, enjoying the effect of her efforts. But Mary was being very noisy, and needed to be punished.

"I warned you Mary," she said. "Now you must suffer the consequences of all that noise."

She picked up her favourite horsehair flogger. It was lovely to look at and felt beautiful in her hand. The braided, sapphire blue, leather handle was perfectly weighted and comfortable to brandish for long periods. The horsehair itself was shiny black and could deliver anything from a course tickle to a sharp, shooting sting, and after years of practice, she could wield it with tremendous precision. She loved it. It was one of her favourite impact toys.

She began to lightly flog Mary's breasts and stomach, building in intensity as she moved all around, reddening every inch of her. Watching as the nipples grew hard and the areolas shrunk to about half their size under the stinging lash. She moved her attention to Mary's lower belly and the intensity of her swings grew to the point where there was a beautiful sharp whooshing sound signalling every lash.

She was carefully landing each stroke so that the tips of the lash were just reaching Mary's clitoris, barely above the head of the vibrator, and Mary's muffled squeals just added to the heat of the moment. She moved to flogging Mary's thighs and buttocks, allowing the strands to wrap around Mary's legs, and increased the intensity of her blows. She was spurred on by her own arousal and by the entire scene, and soon there was no part of Mary's flesh that was not hot, red, and tingling, with the exception of her face. Even Mary's knees and ankles were red.

She moved to focus the lash between Mary's legs at full intensity, flogging her inner thighs, her labia, and her clitoris until Mary's screams of pleasure were ringing in her ears like Church bells on Christmas morning.

She lost count of the number of times Mary orgasmed and she was at risk of climaxing herself which, while pleasant, was largely undesirable when she still had work to do. So she decided it was time to move on. She ceased the flogging and slid the dildo out of Mary, leaving the vibrator strapped in place but turned it off. She undid Mary's arms and legs, then slowly sat her up and removed her gag. She moved Mary's arms to behind her back and bound them there. Then she made her walk to Nicholas and kneel in front of him. She positioned Mary's mouth over the tiny caged cock and said, "Suck that pathetic worm like the hungry cock-sucking bitch you are." She pushed Mary's mouth hard over the cage. Lucky it was a small one, she thought as she moved behind her.

She found the biggest dildo she had in the toy bag and secured it to the strap-on harness she had on over her leather pants. She got into position behind Mary, turned the vibrator back on, and slid the massive cock into Mary's dripping wet pussy to fuck her hard. "That's it, Mary, suck his pathetic little caged cock. Make him want to fuck you like I'm fucking you. Like he never will. Let him feel me pound into you like the filthy whore he married. That's it, come for me my dirty little vixen slut."

Mary orgasmed over and over, long past the point of pleasure. Her legs trembled, her body shook, and she was nothing but a pathetic wet mess of wanton desire existing only to be fucked by her tormentor who was struggling to suppress her own orgasm. The sight of the huge dildo pounding into Mary, the smell of sweat and sex and fear, and the sensation of the fucking were conspiring to bring her undone, but she fought it. She could have her fun when she got home.

She could tell Mary was on the verge of having had enough so she pulled out of her, turned off the vibrator, and pulled Mary's head off her husband's caged cock just in time to see his wasted orgasm slowly oozing out of his confines. She smiled at that. She wasn't the only one missing out, it seemed.

She undid Mary's arms and helped her up onto the bed, making sure she was okay and offering a sip of water which Mary willingly accepted. Mary was weak and trembling, but she smiled. That was a good sign.

She then went and removed the gag from Nicholas and pulled the stockings out of his mouth. She undid his bonds then dragged him by his beard and forced him to bend over the bed, face first in his wife's soaking wet pubic bush.

"Pleasure her the only way you can, you pathetic beast, while I teach you a lesson," she said.

She reached for one of the paddles, a sturdy oak one with decent size holes in it and a good handle, and she began to slap his ample old butt with it. He was so chubby and plump that each time she hit him, his flesh shook as she struck like a bowl full of jelly. She was no longer at risk of orgasm but it was still quite pleasurable.

He cried out with each impact and each time he did she hit harder. His backside and thighs were red and raw by the time he made the connection and did his best to be quiet and concentrate on licking and pleasuring his wife. Once he realised that if he was quiet and diligent, he had nothing to dread, she reduced the severity of the blows. He then seemed to focus and went straight to his work. Soon Mary was moaning and begging him not to stop.

The contrast between the snowy white beard and the hairy black muff was so comical that she laughed when she saw it, in spite of it being a tad unprofessional. But they were so into what they were doing they didn't notice. In fact, they were so into what they were doing she decided it was time to finish. She paddled Nicholas a few more times just to make sure his arse was nice and red and mottled and then she stopped.

She put away the paddle as Nicholas slurped and lapped at his wife's sopping wet pussy. Both of them oblivious to what she was doing. She left the stockings on the bed knowing full well he would use them to jerk off as soon as Mary let him out of his cage. She left the key to the cage on the bedside table as prearranged and left him face down in his wife while she concentrated on packing the gear back into the mobile dungeon.

With a turn of her head, she checked all was well and that both Nicholas and Mary were safe and happy. Then she gave a satisfied nod to herself for a job well done and whistled cheerily as she headed down the stairs and out to her car, feeling pretty good about the evening and knowing she was going home to satisfy her aching wet need in any and every way she could. It was going to be a fun way to see in the Christmas dawn.

Nicolas and Mary were way too far away to hear anything she said and probably way too busy to care that she was leaving. They may have been vaguely aware of it and she hoped they had a good night at the mercy of her experienced hands, but they seemed lost in their own passions when she left them. However, if they had been listening, they might have heard her exclaim as she drove out of sight, "Merry Christmas to all and to all a goodnight!"

Merry Christmas from all of us here at Wolfstone

*****

Sadly, you've come to the end of this book. We hope you enjoyed it. Please consider visiting www.wolfstone.com.au and joining our mailing list so we can keep you up to date with all our latest stories as well as news and special offers for our fans.

We'd love to hear from you. Please tell us what you like, and we will give you more of it. You can contact any of us via our contact page. or our social media links on our website, wolfstone.com.au

Please keep in touch; we miss you already xx

If you have not read our previous compilation, The Red Shoes, we have included a sneak peek below. In keeping with the festive theme please enjoy a tiny peek at A Christmas Carol

*****

Miss Carol held Jennifer's head up and examined her face for what seemed like minutes before she said, "Relax Jennifer. I was only teasing. I am hoping your ambitions might lie elsewhere. And there's no need to be quite so formal; when we are alone, you can call me Miss."

Jennifer wanted to hide but couldn't do anything to break her boss's gaze other than blink. Once she did, the older woman moved her fingers from beneath Jennifer's chin, running the tips of them gently down her throat to the red velvet bow at her neck. Jennifer could feel herself blushing. Her heart was beating so hard in her chest she was sure that Miss Carol could practically hear it.

"I love this bow, Jennifer. It matches those gorgeous shoes perfectly," Miss Carol remarked, gently toying with the strand of velvet at Jennifer's neck. "In fact, I quite like your whole outfit, it shows off your...*style* very well." During the pause in speech, Jennifer felt a tremendous rush of heat flood up from her feet to her face. Miss Carol traced her fingertips across Jennifer's brow and pushed her long dark hair back behind her shoulder.

"You are an exceptionally beautiful girl, Jennifer, and seemingly smart and ambitious. I like those traits in a young woman. But I wonder just how smart and how ambitious you are." The older woman looked into Jennifer's eyes and spoke in a soft low tone. "I wonder if you can see a perfect opportunity when it arises, and if you have the courage to reach out and take it."

Jennifer said nothing at all. She was frozen, trapped in this woman's thrall. Unable to move and not really wanting to.

"I'm willing to bet you have what it takes to take advantage of your current situation, Jennifer," Miss Carol pulled the free end of the velvet bow, causing it to slide undone. Jennifer could now hear her pulse beating loudly in her ears. She had no idea what was about to happen, but she knew she wanted it.

The older woman removed the ribbon completely and dropped it on the desk. She started on the buttons at Jennifer's throat and soon had her blouse undone. She pulled the blouse open enough to expose the tender flesh pressed up just above Jennifer's bra. She smiled a lascivious smile. "Very nice, Jennifer, very nice indeed." She bent forward and kissed the soft bulge gently. "I am about to take you, my sweet girl, and do with your lovely body as I please. I will do you no harm, but I do not like to be interrupted, so if you wish me to stop it is best you say so now. Do you want me to stop, Jennifer?"

The directness of the question and the power of her boss's gaze made it difficult for Jennifer to form a clear thought. But she knew she did not want this to stop, whatever this was, and she knew she didn't want to stumble and stammer and sound unsure, so she gathered all her strength and managed to clearly say, "No Miss, I don't want you to stop."

"Good girl," the older woman said in that tone that Jennifer was growing to love. "I am sure you will not regret your decision...

Want to read all of this story? It is part of 'The Red Shoes'. Available now at Amazon, Barnes & Noble and Smashwords.

www.ingramcontent.com/pod-product-compliance
Lightning Source LLC
Chambersburg PA
CBHW032141170626
46808CB00006B/2330